FINDING LIZZY SMITH

SUSAN KEENE

Other Publications by Susan Keene

Who's Roxy Watkins? (Kate Nash 2)
Tattered Wings
The Twisted Mind of Cletus Compton

Finding Lizzy Smith
Published June 15, 2017

Bent Willow
BOOKS

Published by Bent Willow Books

ISBN 13: 978-0-9898831-6-0

ACKNOWLEDGEMENTS

A special thanks to the writing community of South West Missouri. You are always there when I have a question or concern. You build me up and keep me going.

DEDICATION

*To Imagination: that allows us to find elephants
and teddy bears in the clouds.*

CHAPTER 1

The red dot lingered a bit too long on my left breast or I wouldn't have seen it in the morning sun. In one awkward movement, I jumped, ducked, and rolled, ending under the bench where I'd sat a moment ago. A shot rang out, hitting the concrete seat above my head.

"Breathe, Kate, breathe. You're a detective, you can handle this," I told myself.

My heart beat in my ears. I took a deep breath to calm down. Jeez, I needed to move. The closest tree looked about thirty yards away. The laser sight danced around my knee and lower leg, the only part of me not squished out of sight. As small as I am, I couldn't maneuver any further under the seat.

Someone ran toward me from behind. The laser dot disappeared.

Ryan Meade ducked down behind me. "It's me. Let's get out of here."

No longer afraid, I let him help me. Together we ran to the nearest tree.

"What's going on?" he asked.

I tried to catch my breath and still answer him. "Someone shot at me."

I saw the look of concern on his face.

"Any idea who or why?" he asked.

"No. How far are we from your house?"

"It's a quarter of a mile at the most. Think you can make it?"

"I'm not hurt, just scared."

Another shot rang out. It hit the tree below my left hand. The bark exploded and nicked me below my left eye. Whoever the shooter turned out to be, they either didn't want to kill me or couldn't handle the gun.

Ryan took my hand, and we ran full speed. His stride doubled mine so he half-dragged and pulled me along with him. We zigzagged from tree to bush until we got to the house.

About twenty yards from the garage door, it began to open. He dived under the open door so hard I landed on top of him. He lowered the door. "Did you call the police?"

"No, I was too busy trying to live."

"I need to set the alarms and lock the doors."

I had let my body go limp on top of him. Unless I moved, he wasn't going anywhere. I rolled over on my back, into an empty space and concentrated on calming down. Ryan went into the house. A few minutes later, he walked back into the garage and sat cross-legged on the floor to catch his breath. I moved over and sat up to lean on the truck behind me. "Why were you in the garden?" he asked.

"At three-fifteen this morning, I received a message from Lizzy. It said to meet her in your garden at eight a.m. The message was marked urgent. I waited an hour and a half, during which time, I called, texted, and left umpteen messages. I didn't get an answer. I just started to leave when someone shot at me. Why were you there?"

He looked amused. "It's my backyard. I run the jogging path every morning."

Meade Park was a public garden owned by the Meade Family Trust, which Ryan inherited when his parents died. The park was about forty-five acres. You could enter from Forest Park on the North or Ryan could get to it from his back yard on the south. It was the biggest tract of privately owned land within the St. Louis city limits.

"Well, Lizzy's not the type to make you worry unnecessarily. Any idea what's up?"

"No, I thought I'd find out this morning when I met with her. You spend more time with her than I do. When did you last speak to her?"

Ryan rubbed his hand over his handsome square jaw. "A couple of days ago. She's having a showing at my gallery downtown. We met for dinner to finalize the arrangements. She seemed fine. We were together for hours. I sure didn't pick up on anything."

"Did you see anyone on your run?"

"No. Most people don't know about the jogging path and those who do prefer Forest Park. This area is pretty isolated."

Ryan, Lizzy, and I had been friends since we attended Northwestern, in Chicago together. Ryan, the orphaned rich kid who treated us like family; Lizzy, the art prodigy; and me, the woman who intended to clean up the streets of St. Louis single-handedly. *Funny how things work out.*

Of the original nine friends, there were seven left. My husband, Michael, died three years ago and Roomy Martin, two years ago. Ryan remained close to all of us, but he and Lizzy and he and I spent a lot of time together. Lizzy and I shared a room for three years in college, but we were as different as Alaska and Hawaii.

"Kate?"

Hearing my name brought me back. "Huh. Oh, I'm sorry, just trying to figure it all out."

"It's time you called the police."

"I'll call Roger Simon." Roger and I worked together when I wore a shield. He said he'd take *the rookie* when I came on the force. For the next six years, we fought crime, rescued people, and locked up the bad guys.

Roger came quietly, no sirens or flashing lights to announce his arrival. We walked him and a couple of his CSI crew back to the garden. His men spread out. Roger stayed with Ryan and me to take our statements.

"So your friend emailed you at three this morning?" Roger fished his notebook out of his jacket.

"She sent a text."

"Do you still have that? I'd like to see it."

I showed it to him. Ryan walked around, stood behind him, and read over his shoulder. When he handed the phone back, he gave me the same speech I had given scared parents and grieving spouses a thousand times when I worked with him.

"Kate, it amounts to this: Anyone over the age of eighteen has a right to go anywhere they want with anyone they wish, and they are not obligated to tell anyone about it."

"I know, if they haven't shown up in forty-eight hours the family can report them missing. At that time, they go in a stack with the hundreds of missing persons reports filed every month. Then a detective, who is already overworked, gets the case. Did I cover it all?" I said.

I found the entire process depressing and counterproductive. To find a missing person, you needed to do it fast. The longer they were missing, the slimmer the chance of finding them unharmed.

Roger's men found two .243 casings about two hundred yards from the bench I sat on, and found a slug in the tree we were hiding behind. A .243 was a common hunting rifle with a range of almost a mile if you could figure the angle of the bullet drop, which most decent hunters could. Not much hunting in the city, so this rifle represented something entirely different.

I kept scanning my body for the little red dot. The sun rode high in the sky now, and a laser sight wouldn't do anyone much good. It didn't make me feel any better.

Roger tried to ease the fact that he couldn't help by giving us advice. "There aren't many options right now. You can check her apartment and usual hangouts, find out who she saw and talked to. If she hasn't shown in forty-eight hours, I'll put someone on the case. If you turn something up to make me think this a criminal case, call me. If she turns up, call me. Otherwise, I'll talk to you on Saturday. Feel free to use any of my resources you might need.

"As far as who shot at you, it's hard to tell. We're in one of the best neighborhoods in the city, but it is only two blocks from one of the worst. It might just be random and have nothing to do with your friend or you. Maybe you looked like a victim sitting alone in a park without a soul around. You know better, Kate."

I refused to let him make me feel like a helpless girl. I gave him my best flat-eyed stare—chin on chest, head down, eyes up, unblinking and unfriendly.

"I'd better head to the office. I'm sure my partner is ready to call out the national guard. Oh, but she couldn't do that for forty-eight hours, could she?" I turned on my heel and headed to my car. I left it in the parking lot near the handball courts in Forest Park. I immediately felt bad about how I treated Roger. After all, he didn't make the rules.

Ryan fell into step beside me. "Wait up, I'll walk with you. Today I'll drop by the gallery. Maybe someone has heard from Lizzy, or better yet, seen her. If I learn anything, I'll call you."

"Thanks." I didn't have anything to say. In times of stress, I liked to be alone to think. Sometimes things I didn't realize happened in the moment came to me in the quiet of my office or the car. I felt bad again. After all, Ryan saved my life less than an hour ago. I could, at least, be civil.

We reached the parking lot, and I looked around. The place didn't have a parking space left. People were driving around in circles waiting for someone to leave. Was one of them the shooter?

Ryan broke into my thoughts. "Kate, are you going to ignore me forever? Am I only going to have your attention on days you're being shot at?"

"I'm sorry, Ryan, it isn't you. You know that, don't you?"

"Yes, but it doesn't make it any easier," he answered.

"Time, Ryan, I need time."

CHAPTER 2

There you are."

My partner, Amy Perkins, sat at her desk, slender legs resting on her ink blotter, shoes kicked over to the side of her chair. She stopped filing her nails and looked at me over the top of lime-green sequined reading glasses. "Ever heard of calling to say you'll be late?"

I raised my hand to stop her. "At first it was too early to call, and after all hell broke out, it was too late."

"Is that why you look like you've been playing tackle football? What happened?"

For the first time, I looked down. My jacket no longer had an elbow, my slacks were filthy, and my shoes muddy. It took me nearly ten minutes to relay the events of the morning to Amy. No one had shot at me since I left the police force, and I hadn't missed it. We had a private investigative service and handpicked our clients. If it sounded like it involved someone with a gun, we didn't take the case.

I took off what was left of my blazer. "Any messages? Lizzy didn't call, did she?"

She gave me a knowing look. "No, but Ryan Meade did."

I waved her off, walked into my office and shut the door only to open it again to tell her I was about to take a shower and change clothes.

The shower eased my weary muscles and did wonders for my mood. I slipped on a pair of tailored tan slacks, a black silk scoop-necked pullover blouse, and a dark brown hound's-tooth blazer. Under my coat, as usual, I wore my forty caliber Glock in a shoulder holster.

Our office had once been a bridal store in a strip mall in Clayton, Missouri, a suburb of St. Louis. One of its most appealing features was a shower and changing room in the back of what turned out to be my office. Amy and I each kept several changes of clothes there. We showered when we were late for an engagement or, like this morning, when things got out of hand. It happened more than I liked to admit.

Amy had put a blueberry bagel, cream cheese, and a skinny latte on the desk along with the morning paper. Today the latte was cold and the cream cheese warm. I ate and drank anyway.

I flipped through the society pages looking for any mention of Lizzy. I found something on page three.

Lizzy Smith's new collection of oil paintings will be on display at the Meade gallery, beginning Sunday April fifth, and running through Sunday April fifteenth.

Widely compared to the late Kay Sage for her use of color and texture. It has been five years since Miss Smith has had a showing in St. Louis.

The public can view Miss Smith's work at the gallery on the corner of Third and Collins. Hours are ten a.m. to nine p.m. daily and noon to six on Sunday. Miss Smith will have liberal hours during the event. Please feel free to call the gallery at 555-554-1232 to find out her personal appearance schedule.

No paintings from this showing are in reserve.

Lizzy hated the comparison to Kay Sage, who shot herself in the heart after the death of her husband, in 1963. I had to admit, I could see why they did. Both women painted in vivid color and minute detail. Lizzy, like all of us, wanted to be a one-of-a-kind.

A picture of Lizzy accompanied the article, along with a close-up of a painting, which sold for two hundred and forty thousand dollars, last spring in Amsterdam. Lizzy hadn't changed much since college—a pretty, thin, quiet woman with a sweet smile. Intelligent and strong, everybody loved her.

The strange combination of dark hair and transparent blue eyes gave her an exotic look.

"Where are you, Lizzy?" I said to the picture, as if it would answer me and solve my mystery.

Butterflies flitted through my stomach.

Before Michael died three years ago, I didn't experience fear often, but now I knew the worst thing that could happen: terror lurked in the shadows.

I shook my head. Maybe Lizzy stayed up late and let the charge run down on her phone or didn't realize the time. Another call proved her cell phone still went to voice mail.

"Hey, Liz. Waited for you in the garden. Hope you are okay. Let me know as soon as you get this message."

There were infinite possibilities to explain where she was. I just couldn't come up with any of them. Of course, none of it explained why someone shot at me.

After folding the newspaper back the way I found it, I pushed everything on my desk out of the way, reached under the blotter, and retrieved a picture. I didn't want to make a connection between my husband Michael's death, Roomy Martin's demise the next year, and Lizzy's disappearance. However, of the nine people in the photo, those people closest to me, two were murdered and one didn't make a meeting she initiated. I couldn't help but wonder.

We had graduated from college and headed to the South of France for a wonderful month before following our separate career paths and individual dreams. Before we left, Ryan had someone take the picture.

When we returned, he gave us all a copy, along with his promise to keep us all close and well taken care of.

He did.

We might not all be inseparable, most of us were like the cousins I grew up with as a kid. When I saw them, we took up where we left off, but we all had lives of our own. Lizzy, Michael, Ryan, Roomy, Andy James, and I stayed and had our jobs and families within thirty miles of each other in the St. Louis area. We were more like siblings who shared one parent who was hell-bent on keeping us close.

Ryan had paid for the entire trip to France. At the time, I thought little about it. He had all the money in the world. His parents were dead. We were his family. Those of us left, still were.

The buzzer on the office phone made its freakish sound. Amy wanted me.

"Marsha Sloan is here. Remember, her daughter didn't come home last night, and you know our friends over in Central have the forty-eight-hour rule."

"I remember, bring her in."

I put the picture back in its resting place and straightened my desk.

Within seconds, a distraught redhead with too much makeup and not enough sleep sat across from me. The bags around her eyes were dark, and she didn't get them from only one sleepless night.

She sat on the edge of one of the chairs as if she sat too hard, it would break. Amy lounged in the chair next to her, legs crossed at the knees, those green readers resting on the end of her nose.

"Miss Sloan, I'm Kate Nash." I extended my hand but didn't stand. I had a hang-up about my height. I felt people might not think I was capable if they saw me first and talked to me second—poor body image, I guess.

They said short men have a Napoleon complex. What did you call five-foot, one-inch women who carried a gun and longed to be five inches taller? I didn't know.

"What can I do to help you this morning?"

"Go ahead, Marsha, tell Kate what you told me. I'm sure we can help you."

"My girl, Sasha, she didn't come home from school yesterday. I called everyone I knew. Finally, her friend Marcy told me she saw her get into a red Camaro with a man she'd never seen before."

I stopped her long enough to ask a question. "Where was Sasha when she got into the car?"

"Right outside Normandy High. Marcy said Sasha was laughing and talking to the man in the car. She waved to her friends and then left with him. No one has seen or heard from her since."

"Do you think he is a boyfriend?" I began taking notes.

"I didn't think so, now I don't know. I went to the police and they said she had a right to go wherever she wanted because she's eighteen. This isn't the first time Sasha has done this. They probably think she will come home because she always has. They said I should wait and see what happens, so I called you."

"Does Sasha have a cell phone and a social media presence?

"Yes, she has both." Marsha answered. "She doesn't answer her cell phone. She hasn't answered any of my texts or voicemails. I checked the computer a couple of times, and she hasn't posted on Facebook."

"Okay, Marsha, is there anything else you can tell me about Sasha? Do you have a current photo?"

She handed one across the desk. No ordinary eighteen-year-old here. There would be no problem picking her out in a crowd. On her face, there was a tattoo of a fairy. It began at her neck and ended just under her right eye. A tattoo of a red and black chain circled her neck as far as I could see. It put an unwanted label on an otherwise pretty, redheaded girl with flashing green eyes.

"Is Sasha an only child?"

"Yes, she's the only family I have left. My husband, Matt, died when Sasha was five. I didn't remarry."

"So you raised Sasha alone?"

"Yes, and things went well until she reached high school. Suddenly, she didn't want to fit in. She did everything in her power to make herself stand out. She started staying out all night and hanging out with kids who were already out of school. She put streaks in her hair, pierced places God didn't mean for you to have holes, and got the tattoos you see in the picture. There are more on her arms. They are all fairies of one sort or the other. One is Tinkerbell."

I tapped my pen on the notepad. "I see. How did Sasha pay for this body art? It doesn't come cheap."

"Her grandmother left her money for college. She said she didn't intend to go and began spending it. I tried to stop her, but she turned eighteen at the beginning of her senior year. There was nothing I could do."

"Okay. Don't worry. We've been finding people for a long time. I have several ideas about where to find your daughter. You go home and try to get some rest. We'll keep you updated until we find her. Marsha, I can probably force her to come home once, but the police are right. You can't make her stay. Have your best argument ready when she comes through the door. It might be the only thing you can do."

"Thanks, thank you very much. There is one other thing. What do you charge for your services?" she asked.

"We charge by the hour plus expenses. I don't think there will be expenses, and it won't take much time. Don't worry about it. We can bill you and we have a payment plan. The important thing is to bring Sasha home. Amy will show you out. Try not to worry. Everything will be okay. I have a feeling Sasha is trying to spread her wings. With any luck we can clip them again."

Amy left to show Mrs. Sloan out and came immediately back.

"I know," she said, "find the tattoo parlor that specializes in fairies and knows guys who drive red Camaros. I'm on it."

Amy never took her hand off the doorknob.

I smiled.

We worked well together.

CHAPTER 3

Cases like Marsha and Sasha Sloan's paid the rent. Many cases came to us because of our Clayton address. Clayton was the county seat of St. Louis County. It was upscale and thought of as the best place to hire an attorney or a private investigator. We talked about hiring a full time receptionist but never got it done. Amy liked office work and her organizational skills were ten times better than mine were.

I had more things on my desk than in it and more clothes on the floor of my closet and the top of my dresser than hanging up or in the drawers. I always had several strands of unruly red hair that refused to stay in the scrunches I used to keep it out of my face.

Amy went to college in Southern Illinois, moved to Chicago, and went through the police academy there. She worked two years for the department, but never made detective. A young man she chased into an abandoned building, after a burglary, raped her. She quit the force and moved to St. Louis. She never left a stone unturned or a case unsolved.

I was a fly by the seat-of-your-pants sort of gal. Together, we got the job done.

Amy came back to my office in record time with all the information we would need to track Sasha. Camaro boy turned out to be Camaro man. His name was Randy Davis, a twenty-one-year-old who had a petty criminal record a half-mile long. It would be easier to persuade the Sloan girl to go home when we pointed out her boyfriend preyed on young women. He surely would see the light when I offered to give his name to the police and suggested he began his relationship with the girl before she turned eighteen. I didn't know for sure, but I had a hunch Sasha would be safely tucked in her own bed tonight.

My apprehension about and for Lizzy grew with each moment. At this point, I couldn't do anything.

Amy was ready to work. "When do you want to start hunting Sasha down?"

I stood, opened my desk drawer and took out another ammunition clip for my Glock. I slipped it in my back pocket.

"After I go by Lizzy's apartment and take a look around."

"Want help?"

"Not right now? Where's Digger?"

Amy's dog, Digger, usually stayed right beside her. She and that Yorkie were inseparable.

"He's at the groomers. I need to pick him up by five."

"Okay, you get the dog, I'll make a sweep of Lizzy's, and then we'll decide what to do from there."

"Sounds good. Maybe we should head to Corner 17 before we go snake hunting. I hate to be so close and not eat there."

"Great plan. When is Jake coming home?"

"Jeez, I forgot about him. He'll be in about five. Mind if I bring him to dinner? He's only here until Thursday. They have a break before they head for Tulsa for a best of five with the Drillers."

"No, I love when Jake's around."

Jake Moore, baseball catcher extraordinaire. He played for the Springfield Cardinals and came to see Amy every chance he had. Amy never talked about love or commitment but Jake had been around longer than anyone else I knew. It had been over a year now.

Amy seemed to thrive in the relationship. He came home enough to satisfy her urges and stayed gone enough so she could work, cook, shop, and do all the things she wanted without having to answer to anyone.

When Michael was alive, we loved to be together—I didn't need to start thinking about that now.

Amy and I walked out side by side and headed off in different directions. Lizzy lived off the Delmar Loop. I loved the Loop, a six-block area of vibrant shops, restaurants, and entertainment, actually in University City, which sat on the western edge of St. Louis.

Amy lived in a three-story brownstone on the Southside.

Lizzy's apartment was bigger than most homes. It boasted a coveted bottom floor in Vanguard Crossing. I rang the bell, waited a reasonable amount of time, and then used my key to let myself in.

The place made me catch my breath each time I saw it. The walls in the living room displayed slightly different shades of green, getting lighter as it went around the room. An original Lizzy Smith painting hung on each wall. The walls in all three bedrooms held more of her paintings. Her room sighed sunshine and roses as I walked in. The second bedroom served as a studio and the third, a guest room.

The kitchen was big enough for a full size washer and dryer, an island, a breakfast booth, and a dining room near the patio door. I once counted forty people in there and it didn't seem crowded.

The three full baths, one off each bedroom, screamed luxury. The place looked intact, clean, yet lived in.

I saw no sign of Lizzy. Her purse and car keys were not there and no light flashed on her answering machine. The cell phone charger lay on the dresser. Nothing looked out of place.

I sat at her desk and opened drawers. I didn't find an appointment book, only a flyer for the new gallery showing which began in four days. I walked around and thought of Lizzy. We shared a room at Northwestern. I studied crime and the criminal mind. Lizzy studied color, sculpture, and the arts.

She loved art history and excelled in it. She said she always wanted to be able to walk into a museum and identify the period, the painting, and the artist. She had accomplished her goal, and so much more.

I considered Lizzy an old soul. She walked closed up. That was an odd thing to think, but I always felt she kept her hands too close to her body at all times, as if she didn't want her body exposed to the world. Even though her hair laid in perfect curls down the back of her neck, she checked it with her hand every couple of minutes, as if it might all of a sudden become a tangled mess and she would not realize it.

The only time she seemed relaxed and animated was when she sat at an easel to work. She painted with abandon.

My heart hurt at the thought of her in danger.

I flopped down on the couch and closed my eyes. I had the time to think about all the events of the day. I had the uncanny ability to recall each movement and sound that accompanied an event. All I needed was complete stillness and time. Today, neither of those things seemed to present themselves until now.

Within ten minutes, I had zoned into the events that began at three-fifteen a.m. I was at the point where Ryan walked me to my car when the doorbell rang.

I jumped two inches, stood and drew my gun. Someone turned the doorknob. They tried it. Had I locked the door behind me?

No.

I took several steps to my left so whoever came couldn't see me. Someone stepped in, took a couple of tentative steps in my direction, and then called out in a familiar voice "Lizzy? Lizzy? Are you home?"

I holstered my weapon and walked toward the voice. "Ryan, what are you doing here?"

"I could ask you the same question?"

I sat down again, relieved and aggravated. "No, you couldn't."

"Why's that?

"Because I'm a cop, and I have a key."

"Kate, you're not a cop anymore."

"By my own choice. Stop avoiding the question. Why are you here?"

"I'm looking for Lizzy. After I saw you this morning, I stopped by the new show. I found out no one had seen Lizzy. The paintings are still in the warehouse."

"You said you'd call. Did you go to the warehouse?"

He leaned against the arm of the couch. "I did call. I talked to Amy. The paintings are sitting by the door. They're wrapped, numbered, and packed."

"How did you get in the warehouse?"

"I donate the space to her and I used my passkey."

"Humm."

Ryan moved around to the front of the couch and sat down. "So where is she?"

"I haven't a clue, but I called Roger and he is getting her cell phone records and any credit card transactions or bank withdrawals made since yesterday. In the morning, Amy and I'll start a door to door here and near the Gallery. Until then, all we can do is worry and wait."

"Would you like to wait and worry together over dinner?"

"Oh, my. I forgot, I'm supposed to meet Amy at Corner 17." I looked at my watch. "Is there any way to delay the opening without saying Lizzy is missing? If she is in danger, I don't want media attention just yet."

"I agree. I'll stage something at the gallery that has nothing to do with Lizzy but will cause a delay in opening." He winked. "Leave it to me."

"Thanks. You can join Amy, Jake, and me if you'd like."

"Can I drive you?" he asked.

"No. Amy and I have a case we have to handle after dinner. I need my car."

Ryan walked me to my car, opened the door, and ushered me in. "How long have you been driving this thing?"

I sighed. "You know, you ask that question every time you see it. It's a BMW, I love it."

"But it's a 1978 BMW."

"Dad gave it to me. I can't bear to part with it."

I grinned and he walked over to his shiny black Ford 150, four-by-four quad-cab and climbed in.

I followed him about nine blocks to the restaurant. Had we been on a looser schedule, it would have been a great evening for a walk.

Amy and Jake already ordered for them and me. It didn't involve brain surgery. We always had the same thing, the house special with homemade noodles. My mouth watered.

Ryan flagged down the server and simply said, "One more."

I didn't think I'd be able to eat after the events of the day and worry over Lizzy. But what started out as a quiet reflective group turned into friends who ate and chatted about baseball and Lizzy.

Jake told us he had a chance to play a game in St. Louis while Yadier Molina recovered from an injury in Springfield. He tried not to make too much of it, but fidgeted and grinned while he told us. Seemed he would be in St. Louis about a week and would catch in a series against the As.

My phone beeped that I had a text. I read it once and then held my hand up for quiet. Everyone looked at me as I read it aloud.

Kate. Sorry I missed our meeting. Called out of town. Emergency. Should be back in a week or two. Sorry I worried you. Feed my cat.

In unison, we all said, "Lizzy doesn't have a cat!"

CHAPTER 4

I texted Lizzy's phone again, no reply. I called and left another voicemail.

Now, we knew more. Lizzy could write a message, had enough wherewithal to leave a clue, and whoever had her didn't want this to go public. It wasn't much, but more than we knew before. It was a start.

No one finished their dinner. Even Amy, who could always eat, spent the rest of her time moving food around her plate but never actually ate any.

We left after Ryan graciously paid the check. He said not to be alarmed when we read about the gallery. He didn't actually say he would burn it down or anything, only that it wouldn't open in the morning or the next few weeks as planned.

Jake and Ryan said they would be at the office in the morning to help us in our search for Lizzy. We didn't turn down the help. I avoided looking at Ryan while Amy and Jake shared a kiss before he headed to her apartment. Amy and I left to find Sasha Sloan.

Amy said the fairy tattoos were distinctive to a parlor in the inner city, not somewhere I wanted to be after dark. I put my foot into it, and we sped in that direction. Digger went home with Jake.

When we pulled up in front of the tattoo parlor, Sasha was outside. She stood leaning against the red Camaro talking to some scuz-crud I assumed had been the one who picked her up from school.

I parked with my front bumper about six inches from his and my back bumper against a no parking sign. If he wanted out, he would have to back up. I tried to look big when I sashayed toward him. Amy walked to the back of their car. She ended up standing right behind the bad guy.

He watched her walk until I yelled, "Sasha Sloan?"

He forgot about Amy standing behind him and turned all of his attention on me. He hiked up his pants. "Who wants to know?"

The man's voice sounded as if gravel grated against his teeth when he spoke. He took one cocky step toward me.

I opened my jacket so Mr. Davis could see my Glock. It was impressive—that size thing again.

"Are you a cop?" It was Sasha.

"Private. Your mother hired me to bring you home."

"She can't do that. I'm eighteen."

I pointed to the rag-tag bum who was trying to look like a modern-day movie star. "How long have you known your friend here?"

He had enough gel in his hair hold up a blade of wilted grass and five, no six, gold chains around his neck. His billfold hung from a silver chain attached to a front belt loop. I could see a .22 revolver in his belt.

Sasha popped a piece of gum she was chewing. "About a year. What does that have to do with anything?"

Buddy-boy shifted his feet, moved his legs apart, and put his hands on his hips. I think he meant to intimidate me. It didn't work. "Move on, little lady, we're busy here."

He reached for the gun in his belt.

Everything else happened fast. Amy walked forward as he reached for the gun and kicked him right between the legs. Sasha jumped down to go to his defense. I stepped in front of her.

Damn, I was a fifth degree black belt, and I wanted to show off a little. Amy took him down in one kick. I had to smile.

With my body between his and hers, I leaned down and, in my most stern voice, I told him the truth. "I know your name, and I know the kind of man you are. I hope this is the last time we ever see one another. If we do happen to meet again, it will be because I am testifying with my friend here at your trial for rape and who knows what else."

He still held his manhood in both hands and writhed in pain.

I nudged him gently with my foot. "Do you get my drift?"

He couldn't speak. He could barely breathe.

Amy took Sasha by the hand and put her in the back seat then slipped into the front and snapped her seat belt. I think the girl was in shock because she didn't say another word.

Before I got in the car, I looked back at him. "And don't ever call me *LITTLE LADY*."

I drove to a safer neighborhood and stopped. "Sasha, I don't know you, and you don't know me. What I do know is that your mom saved your life tonight. I don't mean because that jerk would kill you. I mean because you can only lay and run with scum so long before you become scummy yourself."

Sasha looked out the window and didn't acknowledge me.

I got out of the car and opened her door so she had to listen. "Your mom is a one of a kind. She didn't say as much, but I think she didn't remarry because she thought you were so important, she would dedicate her youth to helping you grow up. I know nobody owes another person a damn thing, but we feel you owe your mother respect.

"That body art you have there is forever. Not so bad in the scheme of things. It's common. However, going out looking for trouble is not cool. Are you in love with buddy-boy back there?"

She grunted a yes and looked toward Amy who had now turned around to face her.

"Well, here's the deal. You're going to go home, clean up, help your mother, and go to school somewhere, or get a job. If you do that for six months, and don't go near that scum-bucket, I won't have him arrested and brought up on charges. I can think of about six, off-hand, and that's off the top of my head."

"You can't do that."

"Oh, yes, we can."

I got back in the car and drove to her house. Amy got out and opened the door. Sasha didn't move.

I looked at her in the rear view mirror.

"Do we have a deal? Oh, and by the way, I'll be talking to your mom once a week. If you're taking this out on her, our deal is off, got it?"

I could feel the heat of her anger drifting toward me and see the tears streaming down her face. "Okay."

I reached back over my shoulder and handed her my card. "Okay."

She didn't throw the card down. She held it in her hand as Amy walked her to the porch. Marsha Sloan opened the door as they reached the porch and ran to hug Sasha. It shocked me when Sasha hugged her back.

It was more than I'd hoped for.

CHAPTER 5

My apartment overlooked Forest Park. It was the nicest thing I had. When Michael and I were married, Ryan gave us a twenty-year lease on it as a wedding present. It was on the other side of the park from his house, only about a mile as the crow flew but about four miles if you had to go around.

The apartment was huge. Ryan thought we would have kids so he made sure we had plenty of bedrooms. I used one for an office, another for a closet, slept in one, used one as a guest room, and one was empty. I rarely had guests. I had the entire top floor to myself.

It was great because the only access was the elevator. It had three keys, my mother's, Michael's, and mine. Michael's was still lying on the dresser in the bedroom where he left it to go fishing with his brother three years ago.

In my line of work, people held grudges. A guy was late every night for a month and his wife hired our agency to follow him. We made a report with fifty pictures of him with his tongue down the throat of a buxom blonde, and he was mad at us. He completely forgot he had an affair. We became invasive for following him and ruining his marriage. He followed us home, slashed the tires on the cars, and threatened to do us bodily harm. Yes, the top floor of a building with limited access was right where I wanted to be.

I took a shower, called my mom, and settled in to read *O Magazine* before I turned off the lights. If I tried to sleep with Lizzy on my mind, I would spend the next seven hours staring at the ceiling. A magazine and two glasses of wine were called for in this situation.

Well, it didn't work. Wine, reading, and Mom didn't do a thing to change my focus. I got up, went into the kitchen, got the rest of the bottle of Moscato, and headed for the living room.

Where to begin? First, her phone records, then some door-to-door around the gallery and her home. There were bank records, social media, and twitter accounts I could investigate. I made myself a promise to find Lizzy.

Her message said to *feed the cat*. She knew we would all get the clue. Lizzy swelled up like a toad ready to croak if she stood within ten feet of a cat.

I felt better after I finished my list, but I wasn't sleepy. I went back in my room and took the picture of Michael off the dresser, and hugged it. It had been two years, nine months, and seventeen days since Michael was murdered. I still couldn't wrap my mind around it.

He and his brother Matt were fishing off a small island near Alton, Illinois, in the Mississippi River. They had camped there for a few days and decided to take the boat downstream to Grafton to pick up supplies. Matt said right before they left, the fish began to bite so they drew straws to see who got to stay and fish while the other went to town. Michael won.

It took Matt several hours to dock, walk to the nearest store, buy groceries, and return to the island. When he pulled up to dock the boat, he found Mike lying face down in the sand with a hole in the back of his head. Matt panicked and ran around the tiny island, trying to see what they took with them. Nothing. It seemed to be a senseless, ruthless execution.

Matt called nine-one-one and then sat holding his dead brother in his arms, not giving any heed to the fact that it was a crime scene. I heard the call come in at work and went over to the island on the coast guard cutter with the other officers who were investigating. There were many small sand bars and islands in the Mississippi, and I had been praying the entire time it wasn't one of the men I loved. Once we got there, it became clear the murder had taken place on the Illinois side of the river and I could do little more than watch. The coast guard and Illinois Highway Patrol were taking the case.

I was devastated when I saw Matt holding my husband in his arms, rocking back and forth, stroking his hair. I screamed and, the next thing I knew, I had been carried back to the boat by my now ex-partner, Roger Simon. I didn't go back to the island for almost a year. Then Matt and I finally took the boat over on a crisp fall afternoon so he could show me what happened.

They never found Michael's killer. It happened on a Tuesday afternoon. The island was too far away to be seen from the shore, and the few people on the river that day didn't see anything. The only clue was a fortune from a fortune cookie neatly folded in his front pocket. It read, *He who sees evil and walks away becomes a victim of the evil he ignored.*

Ryan, the Alton Police Department, the FBI, the coast guard, and everyone else involved knew it to be the clue leading to the killer. Problem was no one could figure it out.

It was now a cold case, open, but not actively investigated. The lead cop said it would happen again with the same MO, and maybe they would leave more clues. Meanwhile, I had lost the love of my life, Matt would never be the same, and a brilliant young man no longer walked this earth.

I put the picture back and went back to bed. I faced the wall away from the dresser and chanted my mantra repeatedly until I fell asleep, "I have the strength to do what is mine to do."

I so wanted to believe it.

CHAPTER 6

My feet ached after hours of canvassing Lizzy's neighborhood. No one had seen or heard anything. I got into my car and headed toward the office. Ryan and Amy were both there when I arrived. Amy had been holding down the fort while checking out Lizzy's cell phone records that the police had couriered over earlier in the day. She found two calls from a track-phone. They came from the same number and were untraceable. One was at six-fifteen p.m. the day before yesterday and lasted seventeen minutes. The second one was at seven-fifteen yesterday morning and it lasted four minutes.

Ryan said a woman vividly remembered Lizzy having a lively discussion with a man outside of Starbucks on the Loop. He tried to get her to sit down and talk with him, and Lizzy didn't appear to want any part of it. The woman said he wasn't anyone she had seen before. She described him as medium height, in his mid-fifties, perhaps oriental. He wore dark glasses and a jogging suit. After Lizzy made it clear she didn't want to sit with him, the woman said the man walked off toward the back of the store.

That was two days ago. She told Ryan she would sit with a police artist. I called Roger Simon and filled him in. He promised to get me a copy of the sketch as soon as it was ready. It paid to have friends at Central.

They were discussing a mysterious fire at the Gallery during the night and how lucky it was Lizzy's paintings were unharmed. An investigation by the fire marshal showed it was a short in a light switch. Some minor painting and cleaning and the gallery would be ready to open in a week or two, a month at the most. They looked at one another and smiled at their collective coup.

Everything happened at once. Diane Fields called to say her husband Stephen didn't come home last night and could Amy and I go fetch him?

I'd swear she had us on speed dial. If I were married to Stephen…well, I wouldn't be. Stephen meant well enough, but every time he went out for a drink with people after work, he ended up at Tillie's Strip Bar.

Problem with Stephen was he didn't go to see the girls, he went to *save* them. Next thing you knew, he had followed one home, was buying food for her kids, and babysitting. Now none of that would seem like such a bad thing if Stephen didn't have a wife and four kids under seven at home.

I didn't have time to put the phone back in my pocket before it rang again. It was Roger.

"Don't tell me you have a sketch already?"

"No, Kate, but you need to come down here, now." He didn't sound like his old chipper self.

"Why, what happened? Is it Lizzy?"

Amy and Ryan stopped their conversation and gave their full attention to my phone call.

"No, It's about Andrew James, he's a friend of yours, right?"

"You know he is. Roger, what's wrong with Andrew?"

Ryan leapt to his feet, but I held up a hand for him to wait.

"Nothing I want to discuss on the phone," Roger said. "I need you to come to Central."

"Okay, we're on our way."

Roger didn't ask who *we* were, and Ryan didn't ask any questions either. I had nothing to say, because I couldn't catch my breath until we were about a block from the station.

Amy chose to stay at the office. She did, however, expect a phone call as soon as we found out what was wrong with Andy. I had a sinking feeling it was bad.

I turned to face Ryan "I don't feel good about this."

His knuckles were white from gripping the steering wheel so hard. "Me neither, I haven't felt right since Michael was killed and Roomy's body was found in the river. Suicide, my ass. Now Lizzy's missing, and something is wrong with Andy. Where is all of this going?"

What Ryan said rang true. Michael was an unsolved murder, and Roomy's death was ruled a suicide. He was the happiest man I knew, and now Andy. What had happened to Andy?

I tried to smile. "Maybe Andy has a speeding ticket he needs help with."

We arrived at Central before I had control of my emotions. Ryan helped me out of the truck. The darn thing sat so high I had to slide out of the seat. He took my hand and didn't let go until we reached the station entrance. His hand felt warm and safe. I didn't put up a fight. It was quiet inside the police station. A grungy-looking vagrant type sat on the bench alone.

Roger Simon stood leaning against the door to the squad room as if he had nothing to do but wait for us. "Hi, Kate. Ryan." He reached for Ryan's hand.

Ryan nodded.

If Roger thought it odd that Ryan was with me, he didn't voice it. "Come into my office."

We followed quietly behind. He pulled out two wooden chairs from the corner and sat them in front of his desk.

"What's up, Roger? Where's Andy?"

"I'm sorry to say he's in the morgue."

I must have looked as if I was going to faint because, the next thing I knew, both men were on their feet, standing over me.

"I'm fine." I didn't feel fine, but I wanted to know what happened. Now.

I tried to take a deep breath. I had forgotten to breathe. I was certain that was the problem.

"Andrew James, age thirty-three, was found with a gunshot wound to the back of the head. A cook at Fountain Gardens found him when he took out the trash about six-fifteen this evening. The body rested against the dumpster. His watch, billfold with eighty-four dollars and three credit cards was still in his pocket along with this." He laid a small piece of paper on the desk. I didn't need to look at it. I knew exactly what it said. I recited it aloud as Ryan read it. *He who sees evil and walks away becomes a victim of the evil he ignored.*

The room began to spin. I almost slid to the floor but Ryan caught me.

"Can you get her a wet cloth and perhaps a glass of water?"

Roger was already on his feet as Ryan asked.

I didn't know how much time passed, it could have been a minute, it could have been an hour. It was long enough that Michael's entire murder passed through my mind. Roomy's dead face stared up at me from the icy waters of the Mississippi, and I could picture Andy's body on the impersonal table in the basement. The fog lifted slowly, and I looked from Ryan to Roger. They both wore looks of concern. Ryan was hovering.

"I'm fine." Again, I tried to smile. This wasn't the behavior I usually displayed, and it certainly didn't fit my image as a bad-ass detective.

"Does Linda know about this?" Ryan looked up to watch Roger's face as he answered.

Linda was Andy's wife of six years. They had three small children. I was godmother to one, Ryan, godfather to all three.

"No. We thought it would be better coming from you. Of course, I know it isn't your job anymore."

He was quick to add the last sentence.

Ryan answered for us.

"No, it's fine. We'll go to her as soon as we're finished here. I had dinner with them at the house just last week. Nothing was wrong. Andy would have told me. He was excited about the new clinic and his new partner. It was nothing but smiles over there."

"Did Andrew have any enemies you know of?"

Ryan answered no. I shook my head,

"What did your friend do?"

"Veterinarian." Ryan shook his head. "Can't imagine why someone would kill him. Considering the note at both murders, I wonder if there would have been a note on Roomy if he hadn't been in the water."

Now I felt sorry for Ryan. He mothered us as if we were his children. He had dinner here, was godfather to this child and that one. He flitted between us, making sure we were thriving.

It took several more hours at the station. We went over the crime scene photos with Roger. He let us see the taped interview with the cook who found the body. It all seemed on the up and up.

Finally, before we left, we went downstairs and identified our friend Andrew James. It didn't look anything like Andy, except for his hair. No one could mistake his red curly hair.

A man goes to work in the morning and is killed execution style on his way home that night. He has a strange note in his pocket, the same one as in Michael's. What did it all mean?

By the time we drove out to St. Charles to tell Linda and then stayed with her until her mother arrived from Godfrey, Illinois, it was after two a.m.

When we got in Ryan's truck, I sat close to him and buried my head in his armpit. I was freezing and sweating at the same time. Exhaustion, grief, and desperation fogged my mind. Ryan drove me to my apartment.

I hoped Amy had retrieved Stephen Fields. If not, tomorrow was another day. I didn't take time to think about whether it was right that Ryan was with me. The year after Michael died, I slept with Ryan on two occasions. Both times, it was because I needed to be held and loved. My world had died on an island in the Mississippi river. I had given up my job as a St. Louis detective because my empathy for the survivors of the tragedies we saw everyday haunted me. I worried about children whose fathers were shot, strangled, or died of a drug overdose. I grieved with the widows and widowers of the slain to the point of spending all my money to try to ease their pain and suffering.

I finally quit, flew to Florida, lived with my mother for six months, and tried to get my head back on straight. Ryan came down to see me on two occasions, but nothing happened. We talked about old times, and Michael.

When I came home, I called Ryan to tell him I was back. The next week we went to the opera, had a fabulous dinner at Tony's, and he stayed the night. I hadn't planned on sleeping with him. But in his defense, it wasn't his idea. He remained a perfect gentleman and asked more than once if I was sure this was what I wanted.

It happened again about a year later. Again, I took full responsibility. He was my oldest and dearest friend, a beautiful man inside and out, and available to me. In the fourteen years I had known him, I couldn't remember him ever dating. Lizzy and our friend Sara were on his arm until she got married, then Lizzy and he went to all of the weddings and such.

So here we were again, another scenario much like the others where I wanted him and he wanted me back. We went into the bedroom, kicked off our shoes and jackets, and lay on the bed, exhausted. I turned toward the windows over-looking the river. Ryan lay lightly behind me. He snuggled into all of my bends and we fell asleep.

Ryan didn't move. I couldn't read him. As I drifted off, I heard his breath become even and soothing against my back. I slept the sleep of a person who uses it for an escape, to get away from thinking,

CHAPTER 7

I woke up stiff and startled. I heard Ryan in the kitchen, rolled over on my back, and listened to his movements. When you lived alone, the sounds of someone puttering around the house could be unsettling or calming, depending on the circumstances. In this case, I found it calming. I didn't have time to dwell on it because he came through the bedroom door with a tray carrying two cups of coffee and two toasted bagels with cream cheese.

He set the tray on the bedside table. "I raided your kitchen. Hope you don't mind."

"No, not at all."

Sitting on the bed, he picked up the tray and put it between us. "We need to see if we can get the files of all three murders so we can review the details side by side. Do you think Roger will help us with that?"

I reached for a half a bagel and the cream cheese. "Sure. He made it clear we had his cooperation."

Ryan handed me a knife. "Maybe someone put the note on Andy, because we didn't find one when Roomy was killed."

"What do you think it means?" I asked. "Do you think Lizzy's disappearance is another part of the puzzle?"

He sighed. "I wish I had an answer for you."

I sighed too. "Do you remember any time when Michael, Roomy, Andy, and Lizzy were in the same place? Someplace where they saw something or did something we don't know about."

"I can't think of any one place since we were all in France together. I have a habit of writing on my calendar where everyone is and when he or she is coming home. And, I keep them year after year."

I tried not to give him a strange look but I couldn't help it. I cocked my head toward him, like a cat trying to understand something. "Isn't that a little odd?"

"It might be, but it didn't start off that way. At first, I wrote down birthdays, holidays, and travel plans. There are so many of us, and we keep growing with husbands, wives, babies, and all of their information. I just kept the calendars rather than have to transfer the data year after year."

"Sounds reasonable. I always wondered how you knew so much."

"After Mom and Dad died, I realized you guys were all I had. Being an only child sucks when your parents die together. You're suddenly an orphan."

I reached over and rubbed his arm. "I'm sorry, Ryan. Sixteen is a young age to be on your own."

"Matt Hughes took care of me. He might have worked for Dad, but they were the best of friends. He lived on the grounds and, after a while, he moved into one of the bedrooms down the hall from me and became the uncle I needed but never had."

"He died, right?"

"Yes, four years ago. I miss him every day. In some ways, we were closer than I was to my parents. He was there during the end of high school and through college. He taught me how to handle the enormous wealth I inherited. He was a great man."

We drank our coffee and finished the bagels in silence—that rare quiet that doesn't need words or understanding. It came from mutual feelings of loss and respect.

The phone rang, and we both jumped. I got up and answered it in the kitchen while I made another cup of coffee.

Amy hadn't been able to find Stephen Fields. He wasn't at any of his usual haunts. His wife was frantic. It took me about a half hour to fill Amy in on what happened to Andy. I hadn't called her as I promised. I could tell she was taking notes and trying to find a correlation between Michael, Lizzy, Roomy, and Andy.

We made plans to meet at the office in an hour. The world was still turning and life kept moving. I wanted to stop it and put all my time into finding the answer to who was killing my friends. Was Lizzy a part of this or something random? When someone died, it was difficult to find fault with anything he did before. Not so, with Lizzy, I was beginning to remember some troubling incidents when we were in college and again later. One was as recent as last year. This would have to wait until I figured out what happened to Stephen Fields.

"Ryan, I need to get ready and help Amy find a missing person."

"Not a problem. I'm going to see if I can get a tower number and location for those two calls on Lizzy's phone. Looks like I need to dig back into my files and see when the four of them were together. It could be important, but who knows. It could involve more than just the four of them. We need to find out what happened before we lose any more of our family."

I walked toward the bathroom. "Thanks. I'll catch up with you after I make a little money."

"You know, Kate, you don't have to make money. I can take care of things, and you can put all of your efforts into finding Lizzy."

I gave him my favorite flat-eyed stare, where I looked down but directed my eyes over and up toward him. I was sure he had no trouble deciphering its meaning.

He smiled and walked toward me. "Think I could get a hug? The way things are going, we could both use one."

It felt good to be in his arms.

Ryan wanted me to know he took our times together seriously. I wanted him to know that I was using him when nothing but a human touch could take away my pain. I didn't feel we needed to go over it again.

His hug was warm, sincere, and full of love. Who was I kidding? I wanted more, but I couldn't. I couldn't destroy Michael's memory. I didn't want to let go of it yet. I wasn't to the place where I could see someone else in the role of lover.

As if he felt my thoughts, Ryan pulled back, held me at arm's length for a long moment, and then let me go.

He didn't say anything more. When he got to the elevator, he flashed a smile in my direction and gave a casual salute before he disappeared behind the elevator doors.

CHAPTER 8

I met Amy at the office. We sorted the mail, answered all the phone messages, and kibitzed about the events of the night before. She was visibly shaken to find out another one of my close friends was dead. We went over all I knew, one more time, as much for me as for her.

Problem was we had to find Stephen Fields. Besides, it would help take my mind off the problems at hand while I waited for Ryan to pinpoint an event putting Michael, Lizzy, Roomy, and Andy together. It would also assure we could stay in business.

Within twenty minutes, we were on the way to the Fields' house. There had to be something more going on this time. We had picked up Stephen about a half a dozen times and, each time, the MO was the same. Stephen got involved with other people and forgot about his own family.

The Fields' tree-lined street boasted some fancy homes, mini-castles I called them. I was always surprised at how neat and tidy they kept it with four kids under the age of seven running around with what seemed like no supervision whatsoever.

Today, however, was different. The grass needed mowed. There were trikes and hot wheels in the driveway, and the front door hung open.

As we got to the door, I leaned my head in and yelled. "Diane, are you home?" I could hear her sobs as we stepped in. She sat on the couch in the family room, tears running down her cheeks. She held a baby, one played at her feet, one sat in a chair to her left. I didn't see the other two.

"Diane, what's wrong?"

She jumped at the sound of my voice. "I can't do this anymore. When Stephen does this, I don't know if he is okay or not. When we agreed to have all these children, he promised he would help. We haven't seen him since he left for work on Monday morning." It was Friday.

"Well, I don't want to make things worse, but we haven't located him. He isn't at any area hospital, or at his usual haunts. Is there something else we should know?"

"Not that I know of. Did you check the m—"

She didn't seem to be able to get the word out.

"No. He isn't in the morgue. We'll go out again. I'll do my best to find him."

"If you do find him, tell him this is it. I won't be here waiting if he does it again, and I won't be paying anyone to find him. He can stay wherever it is he thinks is more important than home with me and his children."

"I'll make sure he realizes the error of his ways."

"Do you want me to write you a check?"

"No, we'll bill you."

She began rocking the baby in her lap and gently crying. We slipped out the front door and closed it behind us.

"Stephen Fields, you're a rat," I said under my breath. Amy nodded.

Strip bars never closed. I didn't think they even had locks on the doors. We started at Stephen's favorite. It was a moldy, dark, and dank place off Kings Highway and Euclid. When they saw two women come in dressed in business casual, they immediately tagged us for cops. The bathroom became very popular for anyone who didn't want to be seen.

Amy and I bellied up to the bar.

"Seen Stephen Fields lately?" I asked.

"Don't know no Stephen Fields."

The guy behind the voice had long dirty fingernails, and I wondered if there were any cleanliness rules for titty-bars.

"Come on, Jake. We've been through this before, and you do know Mr. Fields. Don't make me call downtown and get a warrant," I said as loud as I could.

He looked around. Most of the men, who had ended up in the club when they were supposed to be out buying groceries or getting diapers, were long gone. The ones who didn't want us to see them but were not ready to leave were still in the john.

"Your boy was in here a day or two ago. Started telling Milly, our new girl, that she shouldn't be doing this kind of work. Milly's boyfriend was pimpin' her that night. Let's just say a fight ensued. The fella you're looking for didn't walk outta here under his own power, if you get my drift."

"I'm a little slow tonight. Did he leave in an ambulance or a police cruiser?"

"I would say he needed a medic, but I didn't need the trouble so Marty there—" He jerked his head toward the bouncer. "—he put him in his car and dropped him at Barnes Hospital."

"Okay, Jake. Thanks. I'll check it out. If it isn't the truth, you can expect the health department to drop by one day soon. Did you ever think about washing your hands before you stick them in the ice?"

He looked down at his hands and back at me, but Amy was already out the door. I jogged to catch up.

We found Stephen in the trauma unit at Barnes. It would be a kindness to say he was unrecognizable. There wasn't a part of him that didn't support a wound dressing of some kind. His left arm and leg were in a cast.

"Well, Stephen. You really did it up right this time."

He didn't speak. In fact, as soon as he saw us, big tears formed in his eyes, and he turned his head toward the wall.

"Don't you think it would have been nice to call Diane and tell her you are alive and well?"

"I couldn't. I didn't want her to see me like this."

"I know I should feel sorry for you Stephen, but I don't. Amy is calling your wife to fill her in. If she still wants your sorry ass, we will take you home."

"Why would you do that? Call her, I mean?"

"Because she has worried enough and because she pays me."

"With my money," he said under his breath.

"Now, now. This is no time to be that way. I think you might have really done it this time. When we talked to her earlier today, she said she was done with you."

He was crying openly now. Again, I tried to feel sorry for him, but I couldn't. I was trying to choose my next words when Amy came back and called me over for a private conversation.

"Diane said she doesn't want to see him. She said she's going to call his mother and brother and have them deal with him. She said when he's well, healthy, and in therapy he can call, and they'll talk."

I waved my hand like it burned. "Ouch."

"Yeah, but he deserves it."

"Yes, he does. Do you want to tell him or should I?" I offered.

"You tell him."

We walked back and stood by his bed. I relayed Diane's message, and he acted as if he didn't believe it.

"She's been mad before. She'll get over it."

I took a step closer to him. "No, she won't, Stephen. You went too far this time. If you want to try to save your marriage, you had better follow the rules she gave you."

"How's she going to raise four babies on her own?"

Amy put her hands on her hips. "Seems like she's been doing that all along."

"You know, all I ever wanted to do was save those girls from a horrible life."

"Did you ever think maybe you should stay home and raise your kids with some values so they turn out decently and leave saving others to themselves?" I asked.

"But you're supposed to help your fellow man." People in the wrong always tried to justify their actions.

"Stephen, you have to help yourself and your own family first." He turned his head toward the opposite wall and didn't say anything else. I patted his hand. "Good luck."

I guess it was good we found him. Diane would sleep tonight, knowing he was safe and she could let her anger out.

The bad thing was, we didn't spend the time looking for Lizzy, and we still didn't know if the murders of Michael, Roomy, and Andy were related.

CHAPTER 9

Amy and I were on the way back to the office when Ryan called.

I should have pulled over to take the call as I was supposed to, but I didn't. I did, however, put it through the Bluetooth in my car. "Hi, Ryan. What's up?"

"Quite a lot. Where are you?"

"Well, we found Stephen Fields, and we're on the way back to the office."

"Okay, I'll meet you there."

"See you in a few then."

He hung up without a goodbye. Amy and I looked at one another. It was obvious he knew something we didn't.

"Are you hungry?"

"Always," she answered. "Let's meet Ryan first and see what he has."

"Okay. However, I'm in the mood for seafood, and I don't care what it costs. I've been running all day on a bagel and a cup of coffee."

Another one of my flaws was that I could eat anytime, anywhere, and stress only made me want more food. I had to thank my parents for good skinny genes. Otherwise, I could easily put on five pounds a day.

Ryan sat on the stoop. As we drove up, I saw a thick folder in his hand. I recognized it. It came from the cold case files at Central.

I all but jumped out of the car. "What do you have?"

I already had my key in the door, and Amy stood close behind, looking at the file over Ryan's shoulder.

"It's Roomy's file. There *was* a note. They found it in the car, in the side pouch. No one connected it because the same group didn't investigate both murders. The Illinois authorities didn't make the note found on Michael's body public. One of those *withholding details* things. The guys here logged the note but didn't have any reason to check with Illinois because the MO was different in each murder. Roomy was drowned, Michael shot."

I plopped down in my chair in sheer shock. How could it be? Michael, Roomy, and now Andy. And Lizzy? Who knew?

I didn't say anything. I knew he had more to say so I tried to breathe and get more comfortable. Amy sat in a chair across the room and looked as if she were in pain.

"To top that off, Jeffery, who runs the gallery, said a blond man about fiftyish came in three times looking for Lizzy. The last time they got into a screaming match, totally out of character for Lizzy."

He said the man—she called him Spencer—wanted her to paint a portrait of a woman. He wanted her to go to his place and paint it from a snapshot. Lizzy told him no but he insisted, as if she owed it to him. Jeffrey thought Lizzy became frightened because she walked out of the room she and this Spencer were talking in and went to where Jeffrey could see and hear them. He said as soon as this guy realized they were not alone, he left. Jeffrey said that, when the man got to the front door, he turned around and gave Lizzy a hateful look. 'You haven't seen the end of me.'"

"Wow." It was all I could think of to say. "Looks like you've learned more in a morning than Amy and I have in three days. Thank you."

"Remember the man at the coffee shop. It might be the same person. Jeffrey will pull up the tape so we can compare it to the police sketch when we get it. I haven't looked though the calendars yet."

"Ryan, you've done a lot. We're grateful, and hungry," Amy agreed.

"Well, by all means, let me treat you ladies to dinner. What are you hungry for?"

"Seafood, but I hate to ask for that if you're buying."

"Let's go to Hooked. We can take care of two things at once."

Hooked Seafood Bar was, by far, some of the best seafood I had ever eaten. "Sounds good. We need about an hour to put this office in order."

"Okay, I'll meet you at the café at seven-fifteen. Do me a favor and be careful. We don't know if it was only Michael, Roomy, Andy, and Lizzy who got into something bad. I'm going to call the others and put them on alert. A third of us are gone in three short years. We need to figure this out."

My phone rang. I held up my finger, looked at the caller ID, and gave Amy and Ryan a signal to wait. It was a short call.

"It was Roger. Lizzy has been officially declared missing. They want us to drop back and let them handle it. They also want to see the rest of us at the station around noon tomorrow."

"The rest of us, as in me and you, or- meaning, the Group? Why?" Ryan asked.

"I think we should try to reach the Group. We don't know how many of us are involved. Is everybody in town?"

Ryan took his phone out and brought up the calendar app. "Sarah is due back today. She's at a medical convention in Seattle. I'll call her and tell her to be there. Danny and Tim will be at their nine-to-fives. I'll let them know. On second thought, you two wait here until I get back. I would feel better if we stayed together. I expect everyone here by tomorrow morning in time for the funeral."

Amy shook her head. "I'm not a part of this. I think I'm safe, but all of this talk of murder and mayhem, I want to go home to my sweetie. I'll see you two tomorrow."

"Let me walk you to your car." Ryan walked to the door and Amy followed him. "I'll be right back to help you close up," he said to me.

Seemed like forever before Ryan reappeared.

"I took the liberty of calling some of the men I have for security around the city and sent two of them to your apartment building. I have someone meeting each plane to keep an eye on the others while they're in town. I'll sleep better tonight."

"Ryan, I am highly trained and completely capable of taking care of myself."

He walked toward me with a smile I couldn't read. "I don't doubt it for a moment. I'm doing this for me. I don't have any family but you guys. The losses are mounting, and I can't stand to lose any more of you."

"I've lost my appetite." I felt like I was wilting.

"You, not hungry? I can't believe it. Let's lock up and get Chinese on the way to my place. I could use some help going through eleven years of calendars to see if we can pinpoint a time when all of this might have started."

"I don't want to leave my car. Besides, I'd like to see the security tapes from the gallery. I'm concerned about this Spencer. I want to see what he looks like."

"I told Jeffrey I wouldn't need the tape until morning. He's in the middle of fending off people wanting to know when Lizzy's showing will begin. Most of them look around the gallery, notice nothing seems wrong, and want to get on with it. About your car?"

"It's the first new car I've ever had and I love it. It's very dependable. When I had it restored, they even put Bluetooth in it. I don't think there is a new car on the road that can top it. And it's a classic."

He turned out the desk lamp. "I can see where you would be protective. We can take it to the house and put it in the garage where it will be safe from vandals."

I put both hands on my hips and cocked my head to one side. "You're picking on my car."

"Never!"

CHAPTER 10

I followed Ryan to his place. It was massive. I guessed it at twenty-thousand square feet. To live in a place that big would unnerve me. I hadn't been there since college, not counting the other day when I cowered in the garage.

It surprised me when I walked in.

We entered through the kitchen from the garage. It was bigger than my entire apartment, but homey and inviting. He had a small table near the windows and the door to a deck.

A sixty-inch television took up most of the wall to the left, and it looked as if he used the counter for a desk instead of the actual one.

"What are you thinking?"

I got flustered, something I tried never to do. "I was thinking about you, but not the way you think."

"Really? How do you know what I think?"

I ignored his comment. "Why do you keep this big place? It is pretty obvious you only use a couple of rooms."

"I can't sell it. It has been in the family for two hundred years. I might downsize though. I've been thinking about opening the main house to the public and making myself an apartment out of the servant's wing."

"Wing?"

"Yes, wing. I am shamelessly rich, the one percent of the one percent."

"I know, but charming."

"Why, thanks, let's eat while this stuff is hot." It was his turn to be flustered. He began opening the little boxes of Chinese take-out. "Do you want to eat this with chop sticks or a fork?"

"Chop sticks." I said.

"Good."

"I need to wash up. Amy and I spent some time at a filthy strip bar on the north side, and I couldn't possibly eat with these hands."

I held them up like a small child.

"First door on the left."

I couldn't believe it when I looked in the mirror—unruly hair, dirty hands, and a rumpled suit, every man's dream. I did what I could and headed back. I tried never to carry a purse. It usually slowed me down and, if I couldn't use it for a weapon, what good was it? In my front pocket, I kept some lipstick, usually a neutral shade I thought would go with anything. I had never mastered the girly-girl thing.

"Did you find your man?" he asked.

"Yes."

I took a few minutes and told him the story. Then we began talking about Lizzy while we polished off cashew chicken, crab Rangoon, tempura veggies, and shrimp fried rice. We both looked at the fortune cookies and laid them down without opening them. Years ago, we made a game of them, each person at the table read the fortune out loud and added the words *in bed* to the end of it. In college, we got some serious laughs out of it.

Ryan began picking up the containers. "I think there must have been a time and place where Michael, Roomy, Andy, and maybe Lizzy were together and saw something.

Maybe they didn't help when they should have and someone wants to make them pay. Did Michael ever talk about anything like that?"

"No. I wonder if anyone else was involved. I know I was never in a place with any of them where something happened with enough significance to get anyone killed. If Lizzy was involved, why didn't he kill her like the rest? Why kidnap her?"

"There are lots of questions to be answered. I'll get the calendars and we can go through them."

I started to follow him. "Need help?"

"No. You wait here, I'll only be a minute. Pour us another glass of wine."

Actually, nearly ten minutes passed before he came back. When he returned, he held a large box of National Geographic calendars under his right arm. The one on top had 1992 printed across a picture of a rhino with its ivory tusk in the hand of a poacher. Ryan said the one on the bottom was 2016. He sat the box on the desk under the window and stopped to smile at me. "I can imagine you think this is weird. Can I take a moment to explain?"

I began putting the calendars in order beginning with the oldest. "By all means."

"I never felt like I belonged until I met the eight of you. I felt I found the brothers and sisters I never had. This place is big, cold, and impersonal." He held out his arms and turned in a large circle to emphasize his point. "Although my mother and father loved me, they were formal people. We dressed for dinner, talked about opera, artists they admired, and literature. None of the music we discussed ended up on rock radio. No one played catch with me, baked cookies, or taught me how to fish." He turned around and smiled at me. "I am not telling you this so you'll feel sorry for me. I was trying to impress upon you why the eight of you are so important to me. I did my best to keep the nine of us together. Money has never been an object, but I have never had the idea anyone of you were my friend for the money."

"I don't think anyone is your friend for money. We all love you."

Why did that make me blush?

"I began keeping track of all of you like I would my family. I helped with down payments on houses, private schools for kids who weren't thriving, and on and on. So when someone starts killing my family, I get mad."

I couldn't help it. I put my hand on his and squeezed ever so gently. I stood up, we hugged for a long time, and both began to cry. We had held it back all day and when it came, it stayed and stayed.

Once we regained our composure, we began going through the calendars before us. A ski trip to Aspen, but Lizzy didn't go, a shopping trip to New York, without Michael. There was a fishing trip to Alaska without Andy. We got nowhere. Could it have been all the way back at the beginning when we all were kids and went to the South of France for no other reason than to sun ourselves and drink beer?

If so, it meant more of us could be involved.

"I don't remember anything happening in France. No stories about maidens in distress or fights. Nothing," he said.

"I don't either. Tomorrow, after the interviews with Roger, we all need to go somewhere to talk. Maybe one of the others remembers something." Though I doubted it. "I still want to see the tapes from the gallery."

"We'll see them in the morning." He looked at his watch. "Did you know it's three? We have had an exhausting day. I'll drive you home."

"No need for that. I can get in my car here and you have guards at the apartment. What could go wrong?"

"I can't think of anything, but I'm not willing to take the chance. I'll take you home and then I can sleep soundly knowing you are okay."

"What about you? Aren't you afraid?"

"I've lived with the threat of harm all my life. The chance someone might kidnap me loomed over everything I did. It was my parent's worst nightmare. I had a bodyguard at age five. You guys are the closest thing I've had to normal all my life."

"You're a wonderful man, Ryan, and we are all lucky to have you."

He had been moving closer to me the entire time we talked. He was a breath away now, leaned down, and kissed me lightly on the lips. When I didn't move away, his kiss deepened, and I returned it, but I broke the spell, put my hand on his chest, and pushed him away.

"It isn't you. You know that, don't you?"

"How many times have I heard that? " He slammed his hand on the table and gave me a look that said he was sorry he had done it. "Michael is never coming back, and I loved him as much as you did, just in a different way. It would be easier if it were me. I could handle that. I could change or we could talk about it. To fight the memory of a dead man is insurmountable, but I keep trying because I think you're worth it. I've always loved you, Kate. I loved you enough to be happy when you fell in love with Michael. I loved you enough to help you get over him. I don't know how much more I have in me."

I had nothing to say. I was stunned, embarrassed, sad, confused, honored, and tired.

CHAPTER 11

I tried to think about what Ryan had said. It would be easy to fall in love with him. He was right. Michael would never be back. I knew it, but right this instant, the thought crushed me. One day, I would move on, but now, how could I be sure?

Whenever I thought of things I didn't want to deal with I began repeating my mantra until it was out of my thoughts. "I am blessed to have my life. It is wonderful as it is." Tonight it did very little to erase Ryan's kiss, and the warmth of his body; Lizzy, and the fear she must be experiencing; and my dear friend Andy, lying in the funeral home.

After a hot shower and a cup of warm tea, I fell into bed and a fitful sleep. I woke four hours later to my cell phone ringing. It was a short night. The caller ID read Amy Perkin.

"Hi, Amy."

"Hey there. I think I'll call in sick today."

"I'm sorry, what's wrong?"

"You two don't need me. Ryan seems to be doing a fine job on the investigation." Her voice sounded little and uncertain.

"Honey, this is our business. If Ryan's family wasn't involved, he wouldn't be either. We have at least six people on the answering machine who need us. Please don't get your feelings hurt."

"Am I being a baby?"

"Yes, but we're all entitled once in a while. I'll see you at the office in an hour. I'll bring breakfast."

"If you're sure?"

"Of course I'm sure. It's our agency, and Ryan will be out of the way as soon as we solve this. Is Jake still in town?"

"No. He played last night for Molina and went back to Springfield early this morning to catch the team before they head to Tulsa to play the Drillers. Kate, don't get me wrong, I love Ryan. I just don't love him as part of our crime-solving, people-finding business."

"Copy that. He'll be around for a while though. He needs to feel like he's helping find the killer of his friends. That okay with you?"

"Sure, I don't really have an issue with Ryan." She sighed. "Jake and I had words last night about me not wanting to go to Springfield on the days he's in town with the team. You and I know, I'm not much of a baseball fan. Give me a good old-fashioned runaway case any day, and it'll hold my interest, but a pitching duel is boring to me."

"Okay. Don't worry about it. We're just adrenaline junkies of a different kind. See you in an hour."

We hung up. Goodbyes weren't necessary.

When Amy and I opened the office, we divided the workload. Amy had her PI license. She did the office work and handled the new clients. I led the investigations. Everything else, we did together. Her presence and kooky attire made the days bearable. I needed Amy, now more than ever.

I drove out of my way to the Missouri Bakery on the Hill to pick up a caramel stolen, drove through Starbucks, and ordered two skinny lattes, then headed for the office. Amy certainly didn't need anything skinny, nor did I, but like all women, we thought we did. It looked like a parade driving to the office with two cars full of Ryan's men following. Another car with two men in it sat outside the office when I arrived.

Ryan sat in his truck out front, engrossed in a deep conversation on his cell phone. I walked past him undetected and headed for the office door.

Amy was busy answering questions on the office phone.

I set the gooey stolen and coffee in front of her and plopped into the nearest chair to listen.

The conversation went on for a good fifteen minutes. Seemed someone thought his wife cheated on him every Tuesday. He wanted solid proof before he filed for divorce, in hopes of getting custody of his children. Those cases had a tendency to get nasty. I didn't like them, but they paid well and kept me and Amy in the black.

Ryan came in, looking flushed, tired, and worried. He had a coffee mug in one hand and a notepad in the other. He sat in a chair next to me, facing Amy.

"Well, ladies, hope your morning's going well." His voice matched his demeanor.

I glanced up. "What's up?"

"There were three times Andy, Michael, Roomy, and Lizzy were together for any length of time. Once in France, we were all there. Then again, in Aspen in 2004. We all went skiing, but our arrival times varied. The four of them were in the cabin a day or two before Tim arrived. The third time was 2009 when Andy bought out a veterinarian clinic in Chicago. Andy and I drove up. Lizzy had a showing there so she dropped by to help. Roomy drove down from Indianapolis, where he had been visiting his mother, to give a hand loading the truck, and Michael took a couple of vacation days to help drive it back and unload." He seemed relieved to have some kind of information.

"I guess the next thing is to check with the others and see if anyone remembers anything about the trips."

"We can do that after the meeting at Central. Until then, I thought we could go over to the gallery and watch the tapes. Try to find out who Spencer is." He stood up, but I didn't follow suit.

"Amy and I have a couple of cases we need to get started on. I'll meet you at Central at eleven-thirty and we can take it from there. If you get a last name on Spencer or recognize him, give me a call."

"Okay. See you then."

He left without an argument.

Amy and I went through the notes she had made and put them in order of importance. We started with a Mr. Woo.

Mr. Woo had an import-export business in a warehouse on the East side of the Mississippi near Granite City. It was not one of my favorite places. Until they finally built a couple of overpasses, you spent most of your time waiting for trains. Bad for us, but a good place to have a shipping business. We made an appointment with Mr. Woo for Friday. Today was Tuesday.

Next came Leonard Wright, the man Amy was talking to when I arrived. We would meet at the Sunset Motel at two-thirty this afternoon. Seemed his wife's indiscretions took place like clockwork.

The others we lined up for Thursday, Monday, and next Tuesday. I usually loved it when we were busy. Today, it overwhelmed me. By the time, we had returned all of the phone calls and appointments were set, it was time for me to meet Ryan and the rest of our group at Central.

Amy stayed behind to do background checks on our new clients, something we did routinely. Last thing I wanted to do was end up in a lonely office with some hardened criminal who had a six-page rap sheet. This didn't completely rule out the scenario, but it helped.

Ryan, Sarah Delaney, Danny Probst, and Tim Jenkins were already in Roger's office when I got there. There were somber hugs and little conversation. Andy's funeral was tomorrow at one, and we needed to move this along. We truly loved one another. We had gone through the deaths of parents, weddings, divorces, births, addictions, and all the other human conditions and had come out on the other end, stronger for it.

Roger started. "As you know, Andrew James was murdered two nights ago. We have no suspects and no leads. However, there is one clue that keeps reappearing at each crime scene. By crime scenes, I mean the deaths of Michael Nash, Roomy Martin, and Andrew James."

There were audible gasps in the room. I didn't think they knew Roomy was murdered or that the three could be connected.

"At each scene, we have found the same note," Roger continued. "It reads, *He who sees evil and walks away becomes the victim of the evil he ignored.* Does it ring a bell with anyone?"

Ryan and I didn't say anything when he left out the detail about the note being a fortune from a Chinese cookie. It was always good to hold back some information.

A murmur went through the room.

When I looked at Ryan, he appeared to be looking intently at each of our friends in turn. I did the same. All I saw was shock and sadness. I made a mental note to ask Ryan later what he noticed.

Roger cleared his throat. "We have you all here together because we don't know if the disappearance of Lizzy Smith is connected to the killings."

They all began talking at once. Their voices became a loud crescendo that flowed through the room like a tidal wave. Everyone had a question. Everyone had the same question. They didn't know Lizzy Smith was missing. We hadn't told them.

"What is going on? Am I next?"

The sentiment came from each of them. They didn't all use the same words, but I could smell the fear in the room.

Of course, Roger couldn't know. He wanted them to think about anytime they were with the other four and if any unusual event had occurred. Did they walk up on a mugging, or drive away from an accident. He said they should *be careful* and *drop by* his office tomorrow for a *personal interview*. He wanted any memories they thought of by then, written down in their own handwriting. He dismissed us.

Ryan got everyone together at the door. We said we would meet at five at his house. At that time, we would chat about what we knew singularly and collectively. He would have dinner ready. We all hugged and shed a few more tears for our dead friends before we went our separate ways with our private thoughts.

I checked in with Amy. She said things were progressing well with the background checks. On a whim, I asked her to run a check on the rest of our group. If she thought it was an odd request, she didn't say.

All my years as an investigator had led to one persistent fact. No one really knows anyone.

Ryan and I drove over to the gallery on the Landing and spent some time reviewing the tapes of the meeting between Spencer and Lizzy. Whomever this mysterious man was, one thing was for sure, he knew how to keep his face out of the line of the camera. A couple of things were obvious. Lizzy knew the man. He had a wig on, wore baggy clothes so it was difficult to judge his size, and he was left handed. Not much to go on.

On the way back to the office, I took the tape to Roger for him to review. With some of the sophisticated equipment the police had, he might be able to find out more than we did. Ryan headed to one of his restaurants to pick up food for dinner. I hoped to grab a shower before we all met again.

CHAPTER 12

I was the last one to arrive at Ryan's estate. Everyone had on jeans and sweaters. The men sported baseball hats with the logos of their favorite sports teams. The mood seemed much lighter than earlier in the day.

Ryan had laid out a meal for every taste. If you couldn't find something to eat, you just weren't hungry. On the range, there were two kinds of soup and a pot of chili simmering. There were burgers, ham sandwiches, humus, chips, wings, spaghetti, salad, fruit, and on and on.

Everyone filled his or her plate and perched around the room. The women were at the table, except for Sarah who jumped up on the island next to Tim. He was telling an involved story about Michael and Roomy, and the *one that got away*. One by one, everybody quieted down and began to listen. It was reminiscent of the movie *The Big Chill*.

As the evening wound down, my confusion grew. We all had some valid points. Maybe it wasn't a trip. It could have been something as simple as dinner or a ballgame. No one knew anything about a crime or the witnessing of one. We all agreed we were a close enough group we would have known anything important that happened to one or more of us. What a dilemma.

I stayed behind to help Ryan clean up. He had little to say.

"Why so quiet?" I asked him.

He backed up to a kitchen wall and, with his back against it, slid down so his rear-end was low as he rested on his heels. He tented his fingers near his handsome face.

I smiled at him. He looked away, as if he didn't know what to do next. "It's getting so complicated. I didn't think about it being an ordinary evening out with friends when something could have happened. Maybe whatever happened didn't seem important to them. Maybe they angered someone and didn't even know it."

"I know. A thought occurred to me. Maybe Lizzy wasn't involved. I don't think she's dead."

As if on cue, my phone beeped. I had a text message. I read it and then put the phone on the floor and slid it over to Ryan. It bounced off his foot and he picked it up. After he read it, he shook his head. It read: *Didn't believe me? Said I'd be back. Now I'm all over the papers and TV. Not good. Reminds me of 08. Hope u r feeding my cat.*

He read the text again slowly and aloud before sliding the phone back to me. "What does it mean?"

"Damned if I know. I guess she's alive, the kidnapper, if there is one, is upset the police are involved. The cat reference is a way to let us know it's her, and I think 08 refers to 2008 but nothing about that year pops into my mind."

So much had happened in the last six years. I got a sick feeling in the pit of my stomach. It said something horrible could happen, would happen, or did happen and we needed to find out which.

"I don't think we should tell Roger. I think his interference could get her killed. We need to rack our brains. What happened in 08? It sounds like something that made the newspapers."

I checked my phone for the time, and it let me know it was twelve-thirty a.m.

"It's after midnight. Let me take you home. We can explore this in the morning when the newspaper archives are available to us."

"Just Google, Lizzy Smith and 2008 and see what comes up."

"Good idea." He walked to the table and opened his laptop. "This is amazing, 21,894 entries about Lizzy Smith and 2008. Guess we'll start at the beginning."

I walked over behind him, put my hands on his shoulders, and leaned down so my face was next to his neck. We began to scan the page.

Twenty-five-year-old artist Lizzy Smith sells painting for a record $478 thousand. Lizzy Smith books showing in Malan. Lizzy Smith linked with playboy millionaire Tommy Darden. Lizzy Smith, Lizzy Smith Lizzy Smith, page after page, entry after entry.

"We need to actually go to the Post-Dispatch and look up 2008."

"Look up biggest news stories of 2008 in St. Louis area. It will save us a trip." Ryan turned his attention back to the computer as I pulled a chair up next to him and sat down.

"What about Roger and the publicity. We don't want to get Lizzy hurt by having everyone out looking for her."

"Your guy, Roger, seems to play by the book. I can't imagine him putting out a false statement saying she's been found."

"He might not go that far, but he might tone it down a little. Thank goodness you didn't post a reward."

Ryan looked at his feet. "I have it in the works. I just didn't have time to tell you about it."

"Cancel it. It'll have every cowboy in the area out looking to score a few easy dollars. Anymore, looking for reward money is like geocaching, everyone is doing it."

I watched him get up. He looked like a wrestler in expensive clothes. His body said he went to the gym regularly. I'd never seen it or heard about it. His hair curled at his neck in a well-planned casual look. Wealth and charm eked out of him, mostly because he was raised with money and didn't have a pretentious bone in his body. His hair had begun showing a touch of gray a couple of years ago, but it looked sexy on him. Ryan's eyes were his best feature, though. They flashed when he got excited, dulled when he got upset, and ravaged me when we made love. I blushed in spite of myself.

We were getting ready to read the stories we searched for when a terrible sound came from the patio near the French doors. Ryan went to check it out. He couldn't find anything.

The hair stood up on the back of my neck. Instinct told me something wasn't right.

The minutes ticked by. Nothing happened and then every light in the house went out. Ryan got up to see if the streetlights on Delmar were out. They shined brightly back at him. Now what?

"Stay put. I'm going to the basement to see what happened."

He didn't have to tell me twice. Darkness and I had never been friends, and it got worse after Michael's death. I felt myself tense up and tried to breathe deeply to relax. When that didn't work, I fondled my gun.

It took Ryan less than a minute to come back upstairs, but before he did, the lights flashed back on.

"Someone flipped the switch on the electric panel."

"How do you know a circuit didn't get too hot?"

"There's evidence someone's been down there, and it wasn't me. The window on the west side was open and the box that has a wire latch, jimmied. I need to get some men on the perimeter. I usually have the alarm set this time of night, but when I'm up I feel like I'm a big boy and can take care of myself."

He began making phone calls. I went back to the computer and tried to look up 2008 again but the WI-FI no longer worked. I looked around at all the windows and glass around us and gave a shudder. First Michael, then Roomy, and then Andy all murdered, Lizzy missing but sending weird texts, and now someone in Ryan's house. I needed to think.

"We can finish this in the morning. Your WI-FI won't come on and I'm too tired to think. I'm going home." I walked over to a coat rack near the back door and slipped on my jacket.

"I'll drive you. I don't want you to drive alone tonight. If you want your car at the penthouse, one of my men will drive it there. I hired more security to watch the rest of the group, and you." Ryan pushed a button on his phone and two men appeared at the back door. He spoke with them in muffled tones. Then he turned to me. "Doug will drive your car to the penthouse. I need your keys."

I reached in my jacket pocket and tossed them gently his way.

After the men left, Ryan walked over to me and took me in his arms. We stood like that for several minutes. "We had better go." He held me at arm's length and looked at me. "I'd like to stay with you tonight."

"No, it's late and I need to be alone. There's a lot to absorb. I think best alone."

He took my hand, led me to his truck, and helped me navigate the step as I climbed in.

We rode to my apartment in silence. I thought about how nice it would be to have his warm body next to mine while I tried to sort this entire mess out. However, it was a habit I didn't want to get into, in case I couldn't break it later.

CHAPTER 13

Ryan and Doug insisted on coming up with me to check out the apartment. I tried to dissuade them but to no avail. Ryan tried the doors to the balconies. Each bedroom had a small private space of its own, and then off the living room and dining room area a massive deck reached out over the city. Within ten minutes, they declared me safe. They left together.

Instead of sleeping, I grabbed a legal pad from my desk and started a timeline. Michael was murdered July 16, 2011, Roomy on July 29, 2013, and Andy on April 2, 2016. If Lizzy's text was indeed from Lizzy, and the hint '08 meant 2008, what happened then to make someone want to kill them now? There had to be a connection? Michael was a stockbroker at Stiffel-Nicholas; Roomy, an actuary for Met Life; and Andy, a veterinarian. Lizzy painted.

To my dismay, I'd left my laptop at the office. My search for whatever might have happened would have to wait. If it had enough significance, I kept thinking, it would pop into my head.

I knew the answer lie in the fortune-cookie fortune. The fortunes looked real because they all had lucky numbers on the back. Oh, my. Were the numbers the same? Did they mean something? I ran to the living room and grabbed the file Roger had given me. It contained everything from the three murders. Michael's case lay on top. I hesitated several minutes before I opened it. The picture of his body, dead in the morgue lay on top. I turned it over so I didn't have to deal with it.

Michael Eugene Nash, age 29, COD: single gunshot to the back of the head. Tears welled in my eyes. Where was my professional distance? After throwing the file back on the table, I went to the kitchen and made a cup of coffee, took a hot shower, put on my favorite PJs, and, with a new resolve, picked the file up again. This was necessary. Maybe we were all in danger.

I took a deep breath and approached it like a scientist. It was now five-thirty. The sun came peaking over the balcony. I felt good and I was as awake as if I had slept for days. I began. What could I learn from these files if I looked at them like a cop and not a grieving widow or a close friend?

Michael had twenty-six dollars in his front shorts pocket and nineteen cents in coin in his other one. The note was found in his shirt pocket. The shirt lay some five feet from the body. The bullet entered the back of his head and went out through his right eye. Death was instantaneous. There were no signs of a struggle.

His watch was on his right arm, he was left handed, and nothing at the campsite was disturbed, nothing taken, no witnesses. The numbers on the reverse side of the fortune were 8-11-14-26-49-52. Could they mean anything?

Roomy's files stated he died as a result of drowning. There was water in his lungs and multiple bruises on his body. Maybe someone held him under water and he struggled. The coroner's note said his injuries were consistent with his body hitting the pier repeatedly and most of them were post mortem. His wife, Alicia, said he went for his evening walk along the Mississippi river as he did every night. Bo, their Irish setter, always went with him. The dog came back several hours later. They found Roomy's body three days later under a pier nine miles downriver. Later, they found the fortune cookie taped to the steering wheel of his car, which he kept, parked in a garage a block from his house. I panicked when I saw the picture of the reverse side of the paper. The numbers were 8-11-14-26-49-52. Why had no one noticed that before?

Andy's file showed his death caused by a single bullet wound to the heart at close distance. Both Michael and Andy were killed with a 44 magnum. The ballistics weren't back on the bullet that killed Andy. My hands were shaking when I found the photograph of the fortune-cookie fortune. The numbers all but jumped off the page at me, 8-11-14-26-49-52. What did it all mean?

Lizzy was the wild card. What did she have to do with anything? How and why did she send messages? Was Lizzy a good person or a bad person? What did any of this have to do with her? Out of nowhere, exhaustion circled me. I gathered the files and headed toward the bathroom. I splashed my face with cold water. I was shocked out of my concentration by the sound of my cell phone in the other room.

I didn't get there in time. I didn't know who would call me before eight. I checked my caller ID. It was Amy. I called back.

"Hi, where are you?"

"Still at the house," I said. "I'll be there right away. Are we busy today?"

"Not too bad. How'd it go last night?"

"There's a new lead. Well, not a new lead. A lead we didn't notice before." I was babbling. "I'll be there right away. Tell you then."

Now the intercom buzzed. I pressed the button and a fuzzy picture of Ryan came on the screen.

"Hi."

"Hi," I parroted back.

"Can I come up?"

"It'll slow me down. Give me two minutes, and I'll be there."

"Okay."

The image reflecting back at me from the mirror unnerved me. Dark circles ringed my eyes. I grabbed for a ponytail holder and tried to gather as much of my unruly thick red hair into it as possible, grabbed a pair of pale green slacks, and sort of jumped into them with one leg while I looked for a shirt with the other hand. I settled on a darker green one and vaguely wondered if I looked like a leprechaun. Oh well, I needed something to detract from my eyes. This would do it. Folks would be laughing so hard at the outfit they wouldn't notice how tired I looked.

The elevator door sprang open when I pushed the button. Two minutes later, I joined Ryan in the hall.

"You look terrible."

So much for tact.

"Thanks. I needed that."

"No. You look nice, but did you sleep last night?"

"No."

"Well, you wear it better than I do."

I looked him over. He had on a pair of gray tailored slacks that hugged his thighs and accentuated the muscles under them. The sport coat covering his broad shoulders was charcoal and a pale yellow polo shirt peeked out from beneath it. He always gave the appearance of being much taller.

I was secretly pleased he didn't tower two feet over me. "I have so much to tell you."

"You can tell me over breakfast."

I needed to turn him down again.

"I can't. Amy and I have a ritual about breakfast. The first one there gets bagels and latte. Her feelings are already hurt because she feels left out. I don't want to make things worse."

"Okay, I'll drop you off at your office and go eat breakfast. You can do your Amy thing, and we'll talk in about an hour."

"No!" It came out like an order. "Sorry. I want you to come in with me. I've discovered something, and I need your input."

"What?"

"Wait until we get to the office, I can tell you both." I held tight to the files, as if they were precious diamonds.

"Hi, Amy." I said in greeting as I walked into the office.

She was grinning from ear to ear.

"You're in a good mood," I mused.

"Not exactly. You look like a leprechaun."

"Really. Ryan didn't mention it."

I turned around as he chuckled.

She grinned at him over my head. "He wouldn't."

"I'll go change, but only because it isn't St. Patrick's Day."

I started shedding my jacket as she picked up the two lattes from her desk and a bag I figured contained breakfast and followed me to the office. Ryan sat in the waiting room. I flung the closet door open and picked out a beige tailored leather jacket that zipped up the front.

"Better?"

"Much."

"Ryan, come in here. I'll share my bagel," I yelled at him as I explored the bag.

"I'm ready for this clue you found."

"Well, I don't know why no one noticed it before, but the numbers on the flip side of the fortune-cookie fortune are the same on all three notes. The numbers are eight, eleven, fourteen, twenty-six, forty-nine, and fifty-two."

"Do they mean anything to you?"

"Since one of them is an eight, I thought maybe it might represent '08. The only other numbers that could be in a date is the eleven, the fourteen, and the twenty-six, and of course, the eight."

"This could be significant." Ryan pulled the desk calendar toward him and wrote the numbers big and bold with a pen he took from his pocket.

We all stared blankly.

"Wasn't fifty-two your badge number when you were a cop?" Amy asked.

"Yes, it was. What can it all mean?"

"We need to find out what happened on November 14, 2008 or November twenty-sixth. The fifty-two might be your badge number, but it might be something else. I am not coming up with anything pertaining to forty-nine or to fifty-two, if it isn't your badge." Ryan underlined the numbers again and again as he spoke.

"Listen, your gourmet breakfast is making me hungry. I am heading to Freda's for breakfast and then to the newspaper to look up these dates. I'll get back to you ladies as soon as I have something—one way or the other."

"Thanks," we both said in unison.

Amy looked in my direction. "We need to tackle the Wright case today or lose it."

I nodded in agreement.

CHAPTER 14

As if on cue, Don Wright called. "My wife has changed her routine. She said she had a meeting, and I followed her. She's headed in the direction of the Sunlight Motel, right now."

Amy pushed the button to put him on speaker. "Are you sure that's where she's going? There are a lot of things in that direction?"

He was sure and offered to follow her for us so he could be really sure.

"You go ahead and go to work. We're on our way. The last thing we need is for her to see you or your car."

Amy tried to calm him down.

After much talking, he said he would move out of the motel parking lot and wait for us in a park-by-the-hour lot across the street. We talked on the way there.

"Don Wright is sure his wife meets her lover every Tuesday afternoon at three at the Sunshine Motel," she said. "The fact that she's there now throws his theory out the window. Grab the camera from under your seat will you?"

Amy was driving her truck. She loved that truck. Digger was in the back. He sat in an over-the-seat carrier. It allowed him to look out the window without standing up and getting nose juice on the glass—modern technology.

I couldn't keep my frustrations hidden. "I hate cases like this. Wish we could just try to find Lizzy and give Don and his problems to someone else. Unfortunately, Lizzy's case won't pay the bills."

"Speaking of paying the bills, I sent the check for rent, and they sent it back. The note with it said the building now belonged to someone else, and we have to talk to him or her about the new rent. The note said the new owners would contact us in the near future." Amy hated disarray. "Hope it isn't somebody who's going to jack it up on us, or wait several months and evict us because we're behind."

"Can they do that?" I wasn't a money aficionado.

"I don't know."

"I think we both need to think more positive. What's Wright driving?" I asked.

"A 2002 Dodge Ram, black."

"Anyway, back to his wife. This is going to work out better. We missed her yesterday on her regular day, and now we won't have to wait a week to settle it." That was me, being more positive.

Amy didn't seem to believe me. "I guess."

"What does she look like?" I asked.

Amy handed me a picture of a middle-aged woman with salt and pepper hair, thirty pounds overweight, and supporting a tanning booth tan.

I handed back the picture. "This is a joke, right?"

"Come on. We all know love is blind."

"Is this all we have today? Because we need to spend some time trying to find Lizzy."

"I agree." Amy put her hand on mine in a rare show of affection. Her nails flashed with polish supporting American flags on each tip. "What can I do to help?"

"Really?"

"Of course, I loved Michael too. I think if we can find your friend Lizzy, we can find out what happened to the other three."

This conversation was one I wanted to pursue, but we were pulling up to the lot where Don waited in his jacked-up, over-compensating, kick-ass Dodge Ram four-by-four, complete with mud flaps and KC lights. What any man needed with a truck like that in the city of St. Louis escaped me. I saw Amy shake her head.

I got out and walked over to the driver's side window. Inside sat a wiry fellow of about sixty. He had a full head of dyed black hair and wore a western shirt and jeans. I tapped on the window and scared the begeebees out of him. He put his window down—power, of course.

The Wrights had been married thirty-six years, had seven grown children, and Peggy didn't work outside the home. Until about six weeks ago, she didn't go out much, except to garden club and an occasional lunch with *the girls.* Don needed to know what was going on. He didn't think he could survive without Peggy. I told him to go on back to the farm, and we would call him with what we found out. He gave me a strange look and told me he worked for Version Wireless as a CPA. Go figure.

After we pulled onto the lot of the beautiful completely remodeled—according to the sign—Starlight Motel. Amy and I made a big fuss pretending to look at a map. We pointed in different directions, in case Mrs. Wright noticed us. She didn't. She pulled up in front of the motel office in her bright blue minivan and went inside. Almost immediately, she came out again with a key in her hand, got back in the van, and drove to room 112, ground floor, and shut off the vehicle. She didn't get out.

After almost ten minutes another minivan showed up and out popped three other women who were dead ringers for Peggy, one was shorter, two were heavier, they all carried suitcases with wheels, and large handbags. Amy spotted a Michael Kors. I wouldn't know a Michael Kors from a Michael Jackson. Mrs. Wright unlocked the room and everyone piled in.

Strange.

Even stranger was the arrival of five more Peggy clones, two in vans and one alone in a Lexus. All of them went in room 112.

We sat waiting for something to happen and it did. About an hour into the meeting or whatever it was, Domino's pizza showed up with six pizzas and three other bags of food.

Maybe it was an orgy—a food orgy. Amy snapped pictures of each woman as she entered the room, along with the driver of the delivery van and the enormous bags of food. Jeez.

I decided to talk to the delivery driver. After getting all that food, I didn't think they were going to leave the room anytime soon.

"Hey, buddy, want to earn ten dollars."

"Depends."

Kids today. When I was his age, ten dollars could buy a lot of stuff.

"Nothing illegal, just wondering what those ladies are doing." I pointed to the door that just closed behind him.

"Sure, then. It's not like they tip much. Each one gives me a dollar, like it's a lot of money, and they expect me to set the food out on the table and open the pizza boxes."

He stood there. It dawned on me he wanted the money before he gave me the information. Not that I blamed him. I dug in my pocket and handed him a crumbled up bill.

"I think they're scrapbooking. My mom does that and it looks the same as what they're doing."

"No kidding. Have you seen them before?"

"Oh, yeah, they're here every week. I think it is a club. They read minutes and say the Pledge of Allegiance to a little flag they tape on the wall."

"I wonder why they meet here," I said aloud.

"I know that too." He held out his hand and I placed a five-dollar bill in his palm.

"They used to meet at their church, but they felt like they couldn't talk freely about the things they wanted to because the priest kept dropping in and sometimes he stayed the entire meeting. He ate and drank with them, and they couldn't talk about their husband and kids like they wanted. One of their nephews manages this place, and he doesn't charge them because they don't use the towels or mess up the room. You'd think, with all the money they save, they could tip me better."

"Thanks, you've been a great help."

I jogged back to our car and hopped in. "You're going to love this. Seems Peggy and her friends are scrapbooking in there. They do it every week. They don't like the atmosphere at the church where they usually meet."

"No kidding?"

"Yep, I think this is the easiest money we have ever made."

"I'm glad."

"Me, too."

We laughed and giggled all the way back to the office. The hard work came trying not to crack up while Amy gave her report to Mr. Wright.

Now, we had to go back to things that were more serious. Laughing felt so good, I vowed to have more laughter in my life, and why not?

CHAPTER 15

The entire time we were on the Wright case, my phone vibrated in my pocket. I reminisced of a time when there were no cell phones to keep us from filling our moments with what was actually going on, so whenever possible, I ignored mine.

This, however, did not go away. It was Ryan. He had called twice and left two voice mails.

"You rang?" I tried to keep my good mood as long as I could, but, although he hadn't said anything yet, I knew something was wrong.

"Do you know what happened on November 14, 2008? I'll tell you this much, something major happened that I didn't think any of us would ever forget." His voice caught with emotion.

"What, what?"

"It was the night the Jump Club burned."

"Jeez? No kidding? How could I forget? Where are you?"

"I'm at the house, getting ready to go over to Andy's and spend some time with Amber and the kids."

I felt I needed to be of some kind of help. "Want me to go with you?"

"I think she would appreciate that. Besides, we need to talk about that night. Most of us were there, me, you, Andy, Michael, Roomy, Lizzy, Tim, and Sarah. The only one who didn't go was Danny. He had gone to Seattle to a reunion of his Marine buddies."

"Do you think the others are in danger?"

"We can't be sure it's the central event causing all of this, but it sure makes sense, and it explains four of the numbers on the fortune, date of the fire, and your badge number."

"Yes, yes, it does." I didn't say anything else.

"Okay, I am on my way over. Be there in about twenty minutes."

We hung up.

Memories of the night the Jump Club burned rushed into my mind. It was a scene of mass hysteria fueled by loud music, over-crowding, locked exits, drunk patrons, and smoke—so much smoke.

Michael had a date with a girl named Lori Morgan. I remember because she reminded me of the country singer, Lori Morgan. She was petite, pretty, funny, likeable and, most vivid in my mind, she didn't make it out of the club. I was there with Ryan, Lizzy, Roomy, and Andy. We were showing our support to Michael and his new girl. No, I wasn't jealous. At the time, Mike was just one of the guys, and I didn't want to date any of the guys.

After the tragedy, I got to know him better. Lori's death devastated him. Not because he loved her but because he took her on a date and didn't get her home safely. That horrible fire haunted my nights for years and popped into my memory daily for several more. How could I not put it together? Forty-nine people died in the fire.

Oh my gosh!

Forty-nine, another number from the note. Now I was sure fifty-two was my badge, which I threw around a lot that night, trying to find the others, and because I was young and inexperienced. I couldn't figure out what twenty-six represented, but it would come out. Had we all done our jobs, maybe Andy would still be alive, and Lizzy would be in her studio, painting another half-million-dollar picture.

When I heard Ryan buzz the intercom, I had relived most of that night in my head. I didn't want to be interrupted. I wanted to go through it systematically, but it would have to wait.

"Hi, I'll be right down."

All I could do when the elevator door opened and I saw him standing there was to run to him and bury my head in his shoulder.

CHAPTER 16

Ryan and I spent several hours with Amber and the kids. Her and his mothers were both there. They seemed happy to disappear into the kitchen together while we visited with the widow. Ryan gave the kids baths and took them in to their grandmothers for a snack before he read them a story and put them to bed. I could tell he had spent a lot of time with them because they were at ease. He was godfather to all three—Art, three; Allen, four; and Allison, five. They were too young for this to sink in. They were sad because Daddy went to live with God in heaven. Of course, they had no idea what the long-term implication of that entailed.

I drifted off a second and thought about Michael. After he died, I could comprehend what it meant, but I didn't know what it meant long term. Death had a way of making children out of us all.

When we left, Ryan drove to his house. The early spring night air smelled cool and fragrant. He thought a walk would make us feel better. The peepers sang in the trees, an owl hooted from the top of a giant oak. Anyone who talked about the stillness of the night had never spent much time outside.

In reality, the sounds were deafening—one only needed to listen.

Before we arrived, my phone rang. Roger Simon began talking as soon as I said hello.

"I have some news on your friend Elizabeth Smith. We found her car in a chop shop downtown. According to the men who were systematically taking it apart, they found it on the east side with all of the windows broken out. Her purse—minus her billfold, money, and credit cards—was found inside."

"We'll be right there."

"No need. It's not here yet. The crime scene is in Illinois, and they will process the car. You can't touch it until they release it, and they probably won't so long as Lizzy is missing. The officer in charge promised to email me a report as soon as he gets it ready. I'm sorry, Kate, it's not a good sign for your friend."

"No, no it isn't. Thanks, Roger."

"My pleasure to help and I'm sorry about the news."

I hung up and stared at my phone.

"I heard most of it," Ryan patted my hand. "This changes everything."

"How? She's still contacting us with leads!"

"Is she, or is someone playing with us, luring us with vague facts to shift us into a position where we are vulnerable."

I couldn't make the connection. "Why Lizzy?"

"Maybe we should explore that."

"What do you mean?"

"What does Lizzy do or have that would make someone hold her indefinitely yet keep letting her give us clues about what is going on?"

"I don't know." I sighed. "I need more time with my memory bank and perhaps some notes to remind me of where everyone was that night." I leaned back heavily in the seat and fought back the tears. I hated when I did this. I made me look small and weak. My entire life, when I got angry or frustrated, the tears flowed.

Ryan pulled the truck into his garage. "I brought you here to go for a walk. It's peaceful and quiet. Let's go for that walk. Sometimes the fresh air makes a difference in my clarity."

Clarity, the word I used earlier when I needed to think.

The cool crisp night air hit me in the face and forced me to draw a deep breath. Ryan walked on my left, holding my hand. It felt right. The gardens smelled wonderful. He had just enough light along the paths so I could see the flowers tucked into themselves for the night. We strolled in a pleasant silence for a while. I began to feel refreshed and clearer, and then I saw it.

A small round red dot.

It rose and fell in the center of Ryan's chest as he breathed. Oh no, not again! He noticed it a second after I did and shoved me to the ground, throwing himself on top of me. A shot rang out, then another. He raised enough to let me scramble out from under him and hide behind a clump of bushes to my left. Before I had time to wonder about his safety, he slid in beside me.

I drew my gun from my raincoat pocket and saw Ryan reach behind his back to get the nine-millimeter Makarov he wore in his belt. Whoever shot at us had several advantages—the cover of the flowers and trees, the light of the moon, and they knew where we were. We knew nothing.

"Are you okay?" He looked around as he talked.

"Yes, and you?"

"I'm not happy. I pushed the alarm on my phone back there and this place should light up like a ball field during a game in a second. My security guys will be here soon."

It was encouraging, yet not.

I saw the dot again. This time it hovered on my right shoulder. The shooter, now on the other side of us, had a clear shot. Ryan fired in the direction of the laser sight as I scrambled to the other side of the bushes. Two more shots zinged by, and the place got as bright as sunlight. Four men came charging at us from the different directions. They were Ryan's men, and I all but passed out from relief.

It had been a long time since someone shot at me, and now I had been a target twice in the same week. No one shot at Kate Nash, PI, and I liked it that way. I could hear the sirens screaming through the night heading toward us. I slumped against the nearest tree to catch my breath.

Things got chaotic fast. Roger Simon came out of nowhere and knelt by my side. I wanted to stand but my legs wouldn't cooperate. Something about seeing the red dot on my shoulder allowed the picture of Michael's face to flash before my eyes. The whole thing unnerved me. I knew now none of us were safe. We needed to get Andy's funeral over with and get the others back to their respective cities before something else happened. I wondered if anything could save them. I had to keep in mind they were not at the Jump Club the night of the fire.

Ryan acted as if someone shot at him every day of the week. He barked orders to his men who ran off to search the grounds. In the spirit of cooperation, they called over a local city cop every time they found something.

Of course, the shooter had cleared out and all he left behind was a few .243 shell casings, the same as the first time.

CHAPTER 17

The next morning, Amy and I were at the office having our usual breakfast only we were not alone. Officers from St. Louis's finest were outside the building and one of Ryan's men stood near the door. Did it make me feel safe? No.

The memory of the laser on Ryan and me appeared each time I closed my eyes. I found myself looking out the windows for any signs of a sniper. Now I wished we had added blinds to the front windows.

My office was even worse. We were in a small shopping mall. The office had a back security door with one window that opened to the back alley. It had bars on it but one could shoot through bars. I stayed out front with Amy.

After two trips to Ryan's in less than a week, I had been shot at twice. What did that tell me? Stay away from Ryan's. Ryan and Roger wanted us to cancel all of our appointments with new people. Problem was, we didn't know anyone until we got a case. Aside from a few repeat offenders, everybody was new. We chose to go on with our day as planned. Ryan had a bodyguard but that didn't ease my mind either. All someone needed was a good scope and a high-powered rifle to ruin a life.

"Kate." Ryan wanted my attention. I glanced his direction. "We need to talk."

"What?" I couldn't keep the tenor of my voice as soft as I had intended.

"This has gone on long enough. We need to sit down and go over that night minute by minute. We need to find out who was where, who talked to who, and who it trying to kill us."

"I agree."

"Good. I'll be back here at three. I'll have everything we need to get to the bottom of this. Tell me you don't have any new clients today."

"Actually, we don't. Amy and I have some billing to do, and then she wanted the afternoon off. Jake is going to call at two, appears they need to straighten out a tiff they had before he left."

"I'm relieved you'll be reasonably safe until I get back. I'll leave Davis and Kline here. They're my best. Stay close to them."

"Will do." He reached over and kissed me on the lips. I didn't resist. I kissed him back.

Amy and I balanced our books. We still didn't know who to send the rent check to, and I had a twinge in my stomach that the new owner might have something to do with last night. I kept my thoughts to myself and hoped I was wrong.

The morning flew by. I went to Central and borrowed every file I could on the Jump Club fire. I even shared my hunches with Roger who agreed it was as good a place to start as any. I wanted to sit in a room and go through every step, thought, and reaction from that night six years ago. It might be the catalyst to all of this. Too many people died that night and had died since of their injuries and maybe murder.

I didn't wait for Ryan. I didn't know how long he had been standing at the doorway of my office when I finally looked up and saw him.

"Hi," he said.

"Hi," I answered.

He took a step into the room. "How's it progressing?"

I looked in his eyes. "Slowly."

"Can I help?" he asked.

"Can you?" I answered.

He seemed subdued. "I think so. I was there too and I'll have different memories. Where do you want to work on this?"

"At my apartment, where no one can shoot at us or get to us without scaling a sixty-foot wall." I hoped he wouldn't argue.

He reached over and began helping me gather my things. "Sounds good to me. Let's go by a grocery store on the way. I am tired of eating out. Cooking is cathartic, and I'm quite good at it."

I walked through to make sure the lights were off and the back door was locked.

"I'll send Davis and Kline on over to your place to check it out," he said. "Fanning and Johns are with me. They can stick with us."

"Do you think we need them?" I asked.

"Better safe than sorry."

We stopped by a Schnuck's store in the county. They had an excellent deli and a produce department to rival the biggest farmer's market. Ryan filled the cart with anything and everything that looked good. I picked out three bottles of wine—a Robert Mondovi Merlot, a Pinot Gorgio, and a Cabernet Sauvignon.

I sat on the counter in the kitchen and talked to Ryan while he fixed spaghetti and meatballs, constructed a micro greens salad, and made garlic bread. I helped by opening the wine. It felt good, almost natural, to have him there. *Take a deep breath, Kate. It might be the circumstances and not the man.*

"What's the first thing you remember about that night?" I asked.

He didn't look up from his cooking. "How incredibly hot it was in there."

I nodded. "Me, too, then someone screamed and the world exploded."

He cocked his head, and his eyes looked up to the left, as if searching for a memory. "I remember grabbing for your hand and running for the exit. Had we been farther from the door we would have been trampled like some of the others."

I shook my head. "Like Lori?"

He picked up his wine glass and drank half of it in one swallow. "Yes, like Lori."

"When did you first see Michael, outside the club?" I asked.

He finished the wine and held out his glass for a refill. "It was late. He was in the bathroom when it all started and so he stayed there. There was a small window above each of the three stalls. He and two other men broke the glass in them and the twenty or so guys in there soaked their shirts in water and stuffed them around the door to keep the smoke and heat at bay. They took turns sticking their heads out the tiny windows to get a breath of fresh air.

While he talked, I began to take notes. "How about Roomy, Andy, and Lizzy?"

"I didn't see Roomy, Andy, or Lizzy until hours later. Roomy said he didn't know how he got out. He said there was a wave of people making their way to the door, and he rode the wave. He said the key was to stay on your feet. Roomy was a big guy. Most of those who got smashed were girls and small men."

I got up to pace. "Lizzy was up on the dance floor. Andy saw her and took her to the back of the stage where they ran into a chained door. They hid behind the stage until some-one, a firefighter, broke through the door with some sort of tool. It sounded to me as if they survived because they were lucky and for no other reason. Because the stage was raised, the smoke stayed above them."

"I can understand why someone would want to kill me," he said. "The Meade trust owned the building, but the idiotic manager had a five-year lease. He said he chained all the doors shut but the front one because the place got too crowded, and he didn't want the police to shut him down on the most profitable night he'd ever had.

I stared at him. "You didn't run the club. Why would anyone want to kill you?"

He had drained another glass of wine but walked to the sink, rinsed it out, and filled it with water, then turned around. "I know, but people always want to blame the rich guy. If you have a lawsuit, you want to go after the man with the most money. There were eighty-seven litigations against the club. I was a defendant in all of them. What saved me was that the city did the inspections, and Shawn White, the manager and owner of the club, personally chained the exits. Shawn White is doing twenty-five-to-life on seven or eight different charges. When it was all over, I had the building torn down and a park built in its place." He drained the pasta. "What about Lori's family? Did they cause Michael any trouble, or did they sue the club owner?"

I shook my head. "No. Lori was an only child. Her dad died when she was young, and her mom died before anything went to court. Michael said her mom died of a broken heart. There was a time I didn't think that was possible." My head felt heavy and I let it rest in the palms of my hands for a moment.

"Dinner's ready. Grab a plate."

We ate in silence, each of us in our own little world. The food was delicious and warm, the wine cool and refreshing.

I broke the spell by offering to refill Ryan's glass.

"So my guess is that someone got hurt that night and died recently," he said. "A loved one is seeking revenge. Or someone is out to kill all of the survivors. That would be a daunting task since there were hundreds of people in the club that night. My questions are, why wait so long to start killing people? Why kill Michael, Roomy, and Andy over something that happened six years ago, and where is Lizzy?"

"Those are great questions, and I don't have the answers. We know what all of the numbers are but the twenty-six. What could that be?" I hated things I couldn't figure out.

"I don't know. Also, why would someone know your badge number?" he asked.

We were both helping ourselves to more pasta.

"Because I was in and out of there a dozen times, looking for the others and trying to help. Each time I went in, I held my shield up as if it was a beacon so no one would stop me." I answered.

Ryan nodded and continued his interrogation. "Did anyone stop you or ask for help, or does anything stand out about any individual victim?"

"No—yes, wait! There was a girl. She was under one of the tables. Her legs were a tangled mess, and I was sure the weight of the table was the only thing keeping her alive because there was a metal shaft going into her, a little above the waist. I found out later it had her pinned to the floor. She begged everyone who passed by to carry her out. I thought we should wait for the paramedics. I stopped and held her hand for a while. I couldn't budge the table. The victims were dazed and in shock and just wanted to get out of the smoke and filth. I finally had to leave her to go for help. Remember, not only were there people trampled and burned but also, the roof collapsed from all of the water and fire damage. I ran into two different sets of paramedics. They both told me they would come as soon as they could. If I remember correctly, later we found out there was a nine-car pileup on Route 40, a ballgame downtown, and several other things. It was nearly two hours before they could send more help to the scene. This young woman was seriously hurt. She begged me to help her, but I couldn't do anything. The lay people who were helping were afraid to move her. No one wanted to be responsible for killing her."

When I looked up, Ryan had tears in his eyes, as did I.

"Do you remember her name?" he asked.

"No, but she would know mine. I don't know if she saw the others or not. Maybe she died because I didn't help her. I know I was there when the paramedics finally got her out of the building. I remember the medic shaking his head at me, indicating it was a hopeless situation."

"You mean she was dying?" he asked, as if wanting to be clear about what happened that night.

"I don't know. It could have been that she was losing her leg—or legs. So hard to remember, and my priority was you guys. I didn't have the empathy I have now. I didn't know what it was like to lose someone. I played by the book. I tried to show no emotion and not find out any personal details about the victims. Life was so much simpler then," I said as memories of Michael's body lying limp in his brother's arms flooded my mind.

Ryan got up and went toward the living room. "Okay. Somewhere around here, I saw a list of the names of the dead and injured. It was put together later and printed as a tribute in the paper on the first anniversary of the fire."

He found it and we scanned down the names. Forty-nine dead, twenty-six critically injured. There was our twenty-six. We could now account for all of the numbers on the fortune-cookie fortune. It sent a chill down my back, and I shuddered, looking around. I felt as if someone was watching me.

CHAPTER 18

Dew dampened the sidewalks by the time Ryan left for home. We both needed sleep. Andy's funeral was at one p.m. Ryan wanted to get everyone out of here and back to their lives as soon as possible, even though we were pretty sure now that only those at the fire were in danger. In other words, Ryan, Lizzy—if she wasn't already dead—and me.

I couldn't get the girl out of my mind. Eventually, we would find out who she and the other twenty-five were.

Ryan showed up with a car and driver at noon. We were the first at the funeral home after Amber and the kids and the grandmothers. We sat in the front row. The rest of our troop sat in the second row. The room filled up quickly. I tried not to look around but I could tell Ryan had guards at every entrance and exit and several more were milling around outside as we left.

The service was beautiful, yet gut wrenching. We rode to the cemetery in silence. I hated it. It was a typical, horrible, unsettling event. There were many of Andy's clients there, neighbors, and friends of all ages, shapes, and sizes. It took a full forty-five minutes for everyone to park and meet at the gravesite.

About half way into the graveside service, I saw a flurry of activity to my left. There was a man standing at the top of the hill watching the entire proceeding though a huge pair of field glasses. Ryan's men converged on him and then- nothing. Either they had him or he had gotten away. I would have to wait until later to find out. My heart raced as my head pounded. I wanted all of this to be over. I wanted to know why my precious Michael lay in the cold hard ground. I wanted to avenge my friends' deaths, and I wanted to find Lizzy Smith.

We loaded the rest of those Ryan considered family into the limo and headed for Lambert Airport. One by one, we left them at their various ticket counters with teary goodbyes and promises to keep in touch and let them know as soon as we solved the case.

I realized I had lost touch with them after Michael's death. They seemed like a part of the life I no longer had. Partying with them and talking about old times was something I could no longer do—the pain cut too deep. Ryan, of course, would never let them go. It wouldn't matter if they beat their wives, had affairs on their husbands, or moved to Bora Bora. They were his family. I stood back a little and observed him at each goodbye. I could tell he loved and cared for each of them.

The last rays of sunlight were visible when we got back to my apartment. We heated up the leftovers from the night before and collapsed on the couch with a glass of wine. There was no pleasure in it tonight.

Before we finished, Ryan got out the copy he had of the names and ages of the victims who survived the fire. For months after the fire, there were newspaper articles and each of them spotlighted one or two of the injured and told about their lives before the accident.

Jasmine Wu's story was in the sixth expose I read. I recognized her from her picture. It showed her clinging to life in a hospital bed.

Twenty-six-year-old Olympic hopeful Jasmine Wu's dreams of skiing in the 2010 winter games in Vancouver, British Columbia, ended the night of the Jump Club fire in downtown St. Louis. Miss Wu lay for hours in the wet and cold, pinned under a table and the ceiling beam that crushed her legs. A metal support from the stage, pushed across the floor during the roof collapse, impaled Miss Wu, causing her spleen to rupture and doing extensive muscle and tissue damage. Doctors said if they could have reached her sooner they might have been able to save her legs. Jasmine lost both legs above the knee. She is still at the skilled living college in Colorado Springs learning to live independently.

We tried to contact Miss Wu, but she declined an interview. We wish her the best and will revisit her another time.

I had a rush. It started in my feet and flew straight to the back of my head. From there it slammed forward and hit me in the forehead from the inside. Had I caused this? It could be sugar coated until it looked like an M&M, but the truth still hit me in the face. Not only did I cause it, but also I forgot about it. Who was I? What had happened to Kate Nash, the girl who cried at sad movies and fixed broken bird wings? I honestly didn't know.

I am the Evil. Me, the fortune-cookie fortune was talking about me. I wanted to run out to the balcony and jump over. Ryan saw my reaction and held me tight against him.

I sobbed, yelled, and carried on like an outraged hooker who only just realized she was a whore.

I was the one who passed Jasmine Wu twenty times and gave her platitudes about waiting for the emergency workers to remove her properly. My ass should have been sitting on the floor next to her. I should have found a way to cover her up and ease her uncertainty. Oh, my god! I was a monster!

I became physically ill, broke out of Ryan's embrace, and ran toward the bathroom where I heaved and threw up.

He walked to the bathroom door and leaned on the corner of its wood frame. "It wasn't your fault."

I gagged and cried at the same time. "Oh, but it was. I should have gone straight out and found somebody to move that young girl. What was wrong with me? I *am* evil."

"Kate, you were trying to find your friends. They could have been dead. You got help, didn't you? Besides, you were only twenty-seven yourself. You have grown a lot since then."

"Yes, but I didn't insist they go to her. They worked their way to her, and I let it happen. I feel like I was a monster," I insisted.

"You are not a monster. You were in a tragic fire where scores of dead bodies lay around you. You were looking for your family. Anybody could understand that." He used the same tone I heard him use with Andy's children at the funeral.

"Not Jasmine Wu and whoever's avenging her." I wouldn't let myself off the hook that easily.

He stepped closer. "We don't know it's about her."

I took a step back. "Yes, we do, 'cause if it were the other way around, I would hunt her down myself and kill her."

"No you wouldn't, you're upset. I'll let you freshen up."

He left the bathroom. I stayed behind and looked at myself for the longest time. Did I cause an Olympic athlete to lose her legs? Did I cause the death of Michael, Roomy, and Andy? My surroundings were fading. I thought I might pass out. I sat down on the floor for a while and then got up and washed my face. The stress of the last hour had exhausted me. I wanted to sleep. Instead, I dragged myself back to the living room and sat on an ottoman across the room from Ryan.

He began talking. "I guess our next move is to see what happened to Jasmine Wu. Is she mentioned in any more of the articles?"

We each took a pile of papers and began going through them. It was tedious and took hours.

Finally Ryan said, "Listen to this: 'Jasmine Wu, one of the survivors of the Jump Club fire, graduated from the Kansas City Art Institute last week. She said art was her second love after skiing. Her mediums are watercolor and pen and ink. Miss Wu says her inspiration is Lizzy Smith whose work she greatly admires.'"

"Well, there you have it. Lizzy taught at the Art Institute for a while. Let me think…2011 to 2013, and I think she is a visiting professor even now. We've found our connection between Lizzy and Jasmine. We need to know more about Ms. Wu." Ryan actually sounded happy.

Between the stress of the funeral, the revelation of what I had done at the Jump Club, and too much wine, I couldn't keep my eyes open or hold the tears back.

"Go to bed." Ryan got up to help me. "Our bodies react differently to stress. I couldn't sleep if you paid me. I'll be out here reading about our friend Jasmine."

"Are you sure?" I tried not to sound as weak as I felt.

He walked over and kissed me lightly on the top of the head. "There is a sure stress reliever built into every man. Want me to demonstrate it for you?"

"No." It was all I felt like saying.

I fell asleep immediately but, two hours later, I woke up as if I'd been in bed all weekend. Ryan was still at it. Before he noticed me, I studied his handsome face. He got better looking with age. There were maybe ten gray hairs at each temple and minute crow's feet at the edges of his eyes. Whatever he was reading had his attention.

Finally, when I shuffled on into the room, he looked up. "Hi, I didn't think I'd see you until late morning."

I shrugged my shoulders. "For some reason I woke up. I feel like I've slept for days. Who knew?"

"I've been doing some interesting reading. There are over 118 thousand postings under Jasmine Wu on Google. The first ones are all the same. They have name, date, bio, and high points of her career as a skier and a painter. When you get down a couple of thousand you get some obscure references to the fire, the people who were injured at the Jump Club."

I walked down to the end of the couch and picked up Ryan's bare feet. I sat down and rested them on my legs. My cell phone was lying on the end table. There were four missed calls. I didn't look to see who they were from, I guessed Amy.

I closed my eyes and drifted back to the night six years ago when I sealed the fate of my husband and my friends with my reckless behavior.

We were all free on the same night. That in itself was a miracle. Lizzy and I wanted to go to the Jump Club. It was the hottest thing in St. Louis at the time. The club sprawled over about eighty thousand square feet. It boasted a bar, good food, and live bands. The dance floor, suspended about six feet above the tables, seemed to make dancing a spotlight affair. Sometimes there were as many as a hundred couples up there at the same time.

Talking was out of the question at the Jump Club. The music pulsated through the building, and I swear I thought there were speakers in the chairs to magnify the effect. Now, the Jump Club didn't fit the bill if you wanted to talk or be romantic, but this particular night, we were all in a rowdy mood and we wanted noise, bar food, dancing, and drinks.

Michael's new date, Lori Morgan, fit right in with the rest of us. I liked her. Ryan and I had gone to the club together. Andy, Roomy, and Lizzy met in the parking lot at the club and came in together. We all shared stuffed mushrooms, chicken wings, onion rings, and every other fried and salty food on the menu. The band didn't start until nine, and we arrived at seven-thirty. Therefore, we had an hour and a half of food, fun, and beer before it got too loud.

Once the dancing began, we split up. Michael and Lori wanted to dance. Andy and Lizzy followed them up there. Roomy had his eye on a girl who sparked his interest, and Ryan and I sat awhile. I remember the cop in me thinking it was too crowded in the Club. Ryan pointed out the floor, ceiling, the bar, and dance floor were all fashioned out of wood and how unsafe he thought it was. He was looking at it from the view of someone who owned the building.

The club became more and more crowded. If you wanted to go to the restroom, you had to get into the wave heading that direction and surf into it. Ryan was claustrophobic, and we had caught a movement toward the front door. We were going outside for air and quiet when all hell broke loose.

First, it got incredibly hot. I remembered wiping the sweat from my face and reaching down for Ryan's hand because the movement and heat together made me nauseous.

Someone, way in the back of the dance floor, yelled *fire*. Of course, I heard that happened later. I could have screamed at the top of my lungs, and I am not sure Ryan, who stood close enough to grasp my hand, would have heard me.

I remembered the screams came from all directions and the multitudes were running like the bulls at Pamplona. Everyone ran for the front door, and it seemed like several minutes before the music stopped, and I could actually hear anything other than a roar. Ryan and I were only about ten yards from the door at that time. The double doors could accommodate about five at once but there were about forty there at any given time. Screams of pain and panic grew louder, but no one gave an inch. It turned into a brutal, gang mentality-shoving match. By the time we made it outside, my hand ached from Ryan's grip, and my arm felt like it was coming out of the socket. At my size, I would have been one of the crushed women, had it not been for Ryan.

Once we made it outside, we walked across the street and watched while the police and emergency personal ran around trying to help people and take statements. The fire department was there within a minute or two and a minute after that several nearby firefighting districts. In all, nine departments and ambulance districts responded.

It took hours to secure the place and find all of the bodies. Ryan and I had spent our time going from person to person looking for the others. It had been an hour since the last person came out walking on his or her own two feet. I was hysterical, and then in the first light of dawn, I saw who I thought was Andy bending over some people kneeling and lying around a body.

They wouldn't let us close so again. I held up my badge and headed for my friend. The smell of burned flesh, wood, and ash was nauseating. Michael sat on the ground beside a body I couldn't recognize, Andy held on to his shoulders.

"Lori," he mouthed with no sound escaping, only his hot tortured breath on my face.

A young EMT was putting a sheet over her when I walked up.

I moved on, frantic to find Lizzy and Roomy. About twenty yards into the room, I saw Jasmine Wu. I didn't know her name at the time. She got my attention with a small gasp I heard when I got close to her.

"Help, I'm trapped," she cried, sounding weak and scared.

"I'm not a rescue worker, I am with the police. If I tried to move you, I would do more harm than good. I'll get someone for you," I whispered. "I'll be right back."

She closed her eyes and sank back into the pain. I could see a table was crushing her legs and a ceiling beam lay precariously near her head. I moved on.

About forty feet away, two men were working on a man who looked burned beyond recognition. I told them about Jasmine, but it was easy to see they could not leave the man they were with.

"Did you see anyone else in distress?" one asked.

I looked back over my shoulder. "No, most of the people that far into the interior of the club are burned. I didn't see anyone alive past the lady I told you about."

I kept making my way toward the interior of the club. When I got to the back, I could see where the fire department had cut into the doors. Outside, I found Lizzy and Roomy…

Now, sitting in my apartment with Ryan, again I came to the same conclusion. *I was and am the reason my husband and friends are dead, and that Lizzy is missing.* This needed to stop before the killer took Ryan away from me too.

I sat up, only to realize Ryan was sitting beside me. He seemed to be intently watching me, yet he said nothing.

I looked up. I wanted to be honest, but my voice was gone and tears flooded my eyes. I began to sob. Ryan moved closer and held me tight. All I wanted at this moment was to feel alive. I wanted to get rid of the pain in my heart and the searing images burned into my brain from the trip I just took into the past and the fire at the Jump Club.

Ryan seemed to sense my despair. He lifted my face in his hands and began kissing my eyes, lips, and my neck. I kissed him back as I pushed him off the couch, forcing him to stand or fall to the floor.

As he stood before me, I took his belt in my hands but I didn't take my eyes off of his.

"Are you sure?" he said.

"Yes, I'm sure."

The next few minutes were a blur. I undressed him and he me. It was sex for the need to feel alive, and nothing more. Mostly it killed the pain and guilt I felt. The Kate Nash, the one from the night of the fire, the one who didn't care enough to stay with an injured woman, ravished Ryan Meade. I didn't much like her, but she intended to have her way. I hoped she went away soon.

~ ~ ~

Ryan slipped back into his slacks while I put his shirt on. I didn't bother to button it.

We made fresh coffee, scrambled eggs, rye toast, and I opened a jar of orange marmalade I'd been saving and couldn't remember why. We laughed as we cooked. It was playful and needed. We ate as if we were starving and, on the way to the shower, we stopped by the bedroom and made love again.

The Kate I didn't like retreated so far inward I couldn't reach her, so I let her go.

CHAPTER 19

When we came off the elevator, Davis and Klein got out of the car where they waited with Ryan's men, Fanning and Johns. Ryan dropped my hand like a school boy caught kissing a girl on the playground. If any of the four men had opinions about us, they kept them to themselves.

Davis and Klein followed me to my office and the other two went home with Ryan. We were to meet later. If Amy felt left out before, I thought she would be super upset when I got there. She wasn't.

"About time you showed up."

"I'm sorry. We came up with a possible suspect who might be responsible or at least the catalyst for the murders."

"Well, I went to our Wednesday meeting with Sterling Woo."

"Sterling who?"

"Sterling Woo. W-o-o." She spelled it for me.

"Are you sure it isn't Stanley Wu, W-u?"

"As sure as I can be. He gave me his business card," She handed it to me. "I can tell you he is a strange fellow. He has a big office in Granite City in the warehouse district. Everyone had on a suit, and he wore a silk workout jacket and a pair of sweat pants."

The card was plain white with no trim. In block letters, it said Jas-Woo Imports, Granite City, Illinois, and a phone number. I turned it over in my hand. The other side was black. Jas-Woo?

I looked up. "What did he want, and why did you go alone?"

Amy put her hands on her hips. "Really? Have you called in or shown any interest in our new clients in the past few days?"

"But—" I stuttered.

"I'm not saying I don't understand, I'm only saying we have a business to run. Who do you think ran this place when you sprained your ankle last year?"

I plopped into the chair behind me, one of the rare times I had nothing to say. I had a whole lot of explaining to do, and I needed to get my eyes back on the prize. The prize was this business. It paid the bills.

There would be plenty of fodder from which to write my memories when I retired. I loved it, and Amy.

The police were working on finding Lizzy, so was Ryan. My imagination had run rampant mistaking Woo for Wu and jumping to conclusions that everything I encountered pertained to the murders. Five deep breaths later, I looked toward Amy who was staring at me. Every worry line she had crinkled and scrunched up, making her look like a very old lady.

I took fifteen minutes and told her about the funeral and about the odd man on the hill at the cemetery. I still didn't know exactly what happened. I told her everything but the part about Ryan and me. My face heated up as I skipped over it.

"Wow. Do you think this Jasmine has a mom or dad or lover who is revenging her death?"

"No, I don't even know if she's dead. I was going to go to the records building today. Ryan should be here soon."

I thought I saw her face cloud over, but if it did, it was just for an instant, and she recouped quickly. "We can check it out. It's almost noon. I can fill you in on Mr. Woo on the way. Let's take my car, it's less likely to get shot at."

"Sounds good, but the two guards are still shadowing me."

"Wonderful." She grabbed her purse. "I love me some big strong body guards."

We laughed aloud as we left the office.

Amy drove a step-side Ranger pickup. It was metallic and changed color, depending on where the sun hit it. It had a cute little back seat where she kept a special dog bed for Digger. It was unusual for her not to have the dog.

"Where's Digger?"

"I dropped him at the groomer's on the way to work. Mind if we pick him up on our way downtown?" Amy knew I loved that dog.

"Fine with me. I like the little guy."

I could see Ryan's men were about three cars back. I wondered if anyone else followed us. I couldn't pick up on anything. The day couldn't have been prettier, and I was happier than I had been in a long time. I daydreamed and no longer watched for perps, when something came sailing in my open window and hit the console between me and Amy.

"What the—" I caught myself before I said anything off color.

Davis and Kline were on it They must have been watching better than Amy or I. The guys in the car who threw the missile turned right at the next corner. The bodyguards were right behind them. We pulled over and dug for whatever landed inside the car. Amy found it, an old medicine bottle like everyone in the world uses. Inside was a piece of paper. She carefully opened the lid and removed the slip of paper, which she handed to me. I felt the blood drain from my head and I had to fight to stay conscious as I read it. *She who sees evil and does nothing becomes a victim of the evil she ig-nores.* I was sure I was the only one who received the note and lived to tell about it.

"Amy! Get out of the truck and run."

"What?"

"Now! Get out of the truck and run." My feet were already on the sidewalk. I moved so fast, I almost lost my footing. Out of the corner of my eye, I saw Amy move away from the truck. Then I saw a flash. A noise followed as the doors, windows, and seats exploded behind me and a fireball rose twenty feet in the air.

The force of the blast threw me against the building in front of me. "Oh, please, let Amy be okay," I yelled above all the noise. As soon as I got my bearings, I got up and ran in the direction, I had last seen her.

She sat against a wall that encircled a small coffee shop. Debris swirled in the air. People dived under tables or ran for cover. Amy was holding her head in her hands when I reached her. I knelt beside her and grabbed both of her arms. Blankly, she looked up at me.

"Are you okay?" I asked.

"I think so. My ears are ringing and I feel like my back is wet." I leaned her forward only to see an eight-inch piece of the windshield sticking out from her side about an inch up from her waist.

"Don't move! Surely someone called nine-one-one."

Sure enough, I heard sirens.

She reached behind her and came back with a bloody hand. "What's wrong with me?"

I put my hand on her knee. "There is a piece of glass in your side. Don't move. Help is on the way."

She tried to stand. "No, Amy, really, don't move."

Amy began to cry.

"Does it hurt?"

"No." Now she gave a nervous chuckle. "I am just glad Digger wasn't in the truck. I couldn't have gotten him out in time to save him."

I smiled back at her. Paramedics now stood over us. There were four people taking advantage of the warm spring day by having lunch outside. Three of them left the scene by ambulance to Barnes-Jewish Hospital with non-life-threatening injuries. The paramedics checked Amy over for about fifteen minutes before they loaded her up. Seemed more than one piece of glass was imbedded in her body. Thank goodness, none of them hit a vital organ. When I looked up, Ryan stood above me. They let me stay with him under the promise that he would drive me to the hospital. I couldn't stand on my own but I felt it had to do with my ears. The blast still reverberated through my head.

For some reason, all the shrapnel went the other direction. After what just happened, I hated to say I was lucky, but I guessed I was.

When Davis and Kline showed up, they went straight to Ryan. Seems a man paid a guy to throw the message in the truck. He gave the kid twenty dollars and told him it was a gag on his girlfriend. The only conclusion we could draw was that, sometime during the night, someone had wired the truck so it would explode when they detonated it. Whoever did it couldn't possibly know which vehicle we would drive. That made me nervous. Did they wire my Beamer, or Ryan's truck? How could they with guards watching us twenty-four-seven?

The police decided it was possible and towed Ryan's truck somewhere for the bomb squad to go over it. The same thing would happen to my car shortly. Ryan had Davis and Kline take us to pick up Digger at the groomer's and then to Ryan's to get another car. What a mess.

We took Digger to my apartment with some food and water and headed to Barnes to see Amy. It was dark out by the time we were done. My ears were still ringing, and Ryan insisted a doctor see me.

CHAPTER 20

Amy didn't have to go to surgery. The emergency room doctor removed the glass and had her stitched and bandaged by the time we got to the hospital.

"I couldn't call about Digger. My phone was in the seat of the truck. Did you remember to get him?" Amy sounded drugged.

"I wouldn't forget about The Digger. He's at my apartment, fed and happy and sleeping on the couch." I tried to be upbeat.

"Oh, thanks." It came out, "Hokay, shanks."

"My pleasure," I said. "Do you get to go home tonight?"

"Yes, but now I'm scared. I didn't think I was a target. Do you think they'll come after me at my house?" She didn't sound vulnerable often, but she did then.

I looked at Ryan.

"I don't think so," he said. "I think Kate and I are the targets. However, they don't seem to mind if anyone else gets hurt. Do you have anyone you can stay with?"

Amy turned toward him. "I could go to Mom's in St. Charles, but, Ryan, so could they."

He rubbed her arm. "I know they could. I'll have a couple of my men with you until this is settled. Kate and I can drive you to your mom's. That way, we can go by and get the dog. I bet he would make you feel better."

"Thanks, he would."

Everyone knew how much Amy loved that dog. She once broke up with a man she really cared for because he wouldn't let Digger sleep at the foot of the bed.

Roger walked through the door as we were finishing our plans. "Well, you guys sure get around."

"What do you think?" Ryan asked.

"I think someone is serious about killing you two and anyone who gets in the way. Your truck had a pipe bomb attached to the muffler, and Kate's car had some sort of device under the driver's seat. This is not a good situation, and I am placing you under my protection until it's over."

"Until what's over?" Ryan asked. "We don't have a clue what this is all about."

"Well then, we had best figure it out. I want the two of you out of St. Louis, out of the country would be best. And for good measure, take that one with you." He nodded toward Amy.

"Okay, let's just talk this over," Ryan said. "I, for one, am not going anywhere, and I think the ladies feel the same. I have many resources, Roger, and I will surround the three of us with men if I have to."

Roger looked worried. "Does that include a sweep of all the cars and homes until we find out what we are up against?"

"Sure, why not?" Ryan was clearly agitated. I could hear it in his voice. "Amy, I have a new plan. Instead of involving your mother in this, we'll go by your house, get your things so you can move in with Kate. Okay, Kate?"

I was having trouble following the conversation. My ears were still ringing and the parts of my body that had hit the building were throbbing. "Sure, but what about you? You're not safe either."

"Okay, Roger." Ryan turned his attention back to the cop. "We're all three going to move into the apartment. From there, we're going to figure this out and put an end to it once and for all."

I didn't remember anything after that. I must have passed out. When I opened my eyes, I was lying in my own bed. Noises drifted in from the living room. I didn't bother to get up. Never in my life had I ever been as exhausted, confused, and sore as I was then. I wish I hadn't heard them. I didn't want to think about death and bombings and finding Lizzy Smith today. I wanted to sleep, so I turned over, put my pillow over my head, and blocked everything out.

I don't know how long I slept, and I couldn't remember what happened at the hospital. When I did drag myself out, I went straight to the shower and stood there, letting the hot water run over my bruised and battered body until it ran cold.

Neither Amy or Ryan looked up when I finally made it to the living room. Ryan had his head buried in my laptop, and Amy was at the kitchen table with Digger in her lap and a stack of papers in front of her. I shuffled over to the coffee pot and poured a cup before either realized I was there.

"Hi," Amy said.

"Hi." I pulled the chair out across the table from her and sat down. "What are you working on?"

"I'm looking at the reports from the fire. Ryan called one of his friends and, viola, these babies showed up about an hour later." She made a sweeping gesture with her hand. "It's gruesome reading. How does it feel to sleep around the clock?"

"Did I? I had no idea."

"Almost." Ryan came over and sat with us. "It's almost three. You fainted at about eight last evening so you have several more hours if you need them." He grinned at me. "Are you feeling better?"

I yawned. "Yes. I heard you both talking out here earlier and I felt disloyal, for a moment, for not coming out, but I just couldn't."

Ryan smiled at Amy. "I understand."

"So do. I," she added.

Ryan rubbed his head. "I just called Louis Pizza and a couple of the men went over to pick it up. I hope you're hungry."

"Starved." I nodded toward the laptop on the coffee table. "What are you working on?"

"Trying to find some information about Jasmine Wu. I don't know if we're going in the right direction because I can't find a record of her death. It's as if she dropped out of sight. 'Poof,'" he breathed, barely audible.

I shook my head, hoping to clear the fog. It only made it hurt worse. "How long ago?"

Ryan put both hands on the counter and leaned forward. "That's the strange thing. No credit card charges or cell phone records, but, also, no death notice or death certificate. I can, however, pin it down to within four months of Michael's murder."

"So we think it has something to do with her," Amy said.

I needed to lie down again. "Do you think something happened, and she got worse?"

"It was six months before the first killing that the last Wu painting sold." Ryan seemed excited. "We've got our first solid lead."

"This is all very strange," I said.

About then the buzzer sounded, and we all looked toward the elevator.

"That would be Doug with the pizzas and beer. I'll get it." Ryan walked toward the elevator, and I got up to get plates and napkins.

Amy followed along to help, and Digger lapped up water they had put down for him in the kitchen.

"I need to take the dog out."

"No." Ryan said flatly. "Doug will be up in a minute. He'll do it. I don't want you out."

Amy rose. "Okay, let me get his lead," she said, heading for the guest room.

I could hear Ryan chatting with his security man, asking him to walk the dog. I noticed early on in my friendship with Ryan that he never told anyone who worked for him to do anything. He always asked politely and said thank you. Another mark in the plus column for him. I ran into many rich people during my years in the public service and I knew this was not the norm.

We must have been hungry. The three of us polished off two large pizzas and several beers. I felt renewed from the food and mellowed from the beer.

After Doug brought the dog back upstairs and gave a quick report on the dog's business and the business of the day, he left. We all sat in the living room and discussed the evening before and what they had learned. I just listened.

The four people from the restaurant had been treated and released. They had all given carbon copy reports to the police about what they had seen and heard. Ryan and Amy assured me that I was awake for the entire event. I didn't remember any of it.

According to them, the hospital checked me over and dispensed some medicine for my ears. The ER doctor said it could take weeks before the ringing completely went away. He must have been wrong because it was barely noticeable now.

The young man who threw the canister was in lock-up, while they did a background check and found out if his story was true. No one knew who was actually behind the bombs—another dead end.

Lizzy's car was processed. The only fingerprints in it were hers. The police had a surveillance unit at her apartment. There was no other news, good or bad, about her. The Illinois State Police went door to door in the neighborhood where they found her car. No one saw anything. If they did, they weren't telling.

Amy groaned as she got up from the couch.

"Does it hurt pretty bad?" I asked.

"No. Luckily, the glass didn't go in very far. It's just hard to rest, and if I forget and lean back, I rub the stitches." She walked like the glass might still be in her.

"Ouch." I said.

"I'll live. My biggest concern was my mom. They released our names to the media a few hours after the bombing. I was afraid she would hear about it before I had a chance to tell her I was all right. I would imagine our cell phones are in a million tiny pieces."

"I took the liberty of ordering you both new phones," Ryan said. "Doug will bring them as soon as he can. Worst thing is not having the numbers and names you need."

"I have mine backed up on the office computer. You do too, don't you, Amy?" I asked.

"Sure do, but I sure feel lost without it," she said.

"What do you think happened to the Wu woman?" I asked.

"I don't know," he said, "but I think our next step is to find out who her relatives are, find out why no one has seen or heard from her in over three years."

"Odd," I said.

Amy tried to get comfortable. "Down right creepy."

"When I Google her, her relatives come up as Stanley Wu, Martha Wu, Daniel Wu, Sammy Johnson, and Donald Rain."

I looked at Amy. "Don't you think it odd that you went to see a Sterling Woo? Too close for comfort for me. Maybe he was trying to get information, or thought we would all come together and he could kill us."

"Don't let your imagination run wild," Amy warned. "Why wouldn't he just say his name was Stanley Wu? We wouldn't know about his daughter. It's all too vague to put together."

Ryan was listening but his hands were flying over the keyboard on my laptop. "There's no listing for a Sterling Woo in St. Louis or on the East side."

"Try JasWoo Imports," Amy said.

Ryan looked up from the computer. "No, nothing. There is, however, a Stanley Wu Enterprises in Granite City."

I moved over next to Ryan. "What do they do? Can you pull up a business profile?"

"I'm sure I can," he answered.

While we waited, Amy played with Digger, I got up, cleaned up our pizza mess, and wiped off the counters in the kitchen. I wasn't all that neat but, after all, I had company.

"I have it." He beckoned us over to him. "Stanley Wu Enterprises, Importers of fine Chinese products. Paintings by modern Chinese masters, Wang Zhen, Wu Guanzhong, Chen Shizehg, and American-born Chinese painter Jasmine Wu. Sculptures by detained Chinese artist Ai Wei Wei.

"'We also offer the Hongqi Fifteen luxury sedan, Beluga Caviar, and the Prolly grille. We have also added Panda Tea and Kou Chun Cha mouth-lip tea, picked by the mouths of virgins.'"

Amy laughed. "You made that last part up."

Ryan grinned. "No, I swear, it's right here, come look."

I did and it was. "Do they give an address?"

He pulled up a map. "Yes. It's in the 1500 block of West First Street."

"Amy, what is the address where you visited Sterling Woo?" I knew it wasn't a fluke.

I looked at Amy just in time to see all of the color drain from her face as she read from the business card. "1509 West First Street, in Granite City."

"Okay, what's this all about?" Ryan asked.

"After the shooting in your garden," Amy said, "we got three or four new client requests. Kate was busy with Andy's funeral and trying to stay alive. I went through the new list and did the usual background checks. Sterling Woo passed everything. Now I have to admit, we don't go real deep. So I went to talk to him. He wants us to watch his business because he thinks someone is stealing. Said he wanted to be discreet so his employees wouldn't know he suspected anything was going on."

"Why wouldn't he use his real name, I wonder?"

"Got me. He's a strange man. The offices are on the second floor of a warehouse I would guess at least a million square feet. He had several clerks and a woman who seemed to be his personal assistant. Of course, I only called him Mr. Woo, so if it is indeed Mr. Wu, they wouldn't know the difference and neither would I."

Amy made sense.

The detective in me took over. "What else do you remember about him?"

"Well, he stuck out like a sore thumb. Everybody in the place was dressed up but him. He had on a silk running jacket and sweatpants. Looked like he just got off the running trail, but his belly showed he has probably never run a step in his life. He's about five feet, six inches and has light hair. Chinese usually don't have light hair so I'm guessing it's dyed."

Ryan got up and retrieved a photo from a file on the dining table. "I realize this is from the back, but could it be your Mr. Woo?"

"Yes, I think it could. Where did you get this?" Amy asked.

Ryan tapped the picture with the tips of his fingers. "It's from the gallery, the day Lizzy went missing. She had words with this gentleman before she disappeared."

"What are we going to do? Should we call Roger and get the police involved?" I was ready to go back to bed.

Ryan took out his cell phone. "No, not yet. Tomorrow you'll call Mr. Woo, and let him hire you to watch his business. Meanwhile, I'll get a couple of my men to watch him. We'll find out where he lives. I think he's the answer to finding Lizzy."

Amy and I nodded in agreement.

We were sitting around resting, each of us content to sip the glass of wine I poured for us, when the intercom came on, and we all jumped. "I'll get it." I said.

"Better let me. It's after eleven. If it isn't one of my men, then it's someone we don't want to see anyway." He walked over and pushed the button so he could talk. I couldn't hear everything, but a few minutes later Doug was standing in the entryway with two boxes and the office computer. Ryan came back with everything and sat it on the dining room table. "New phones and the computer from the office so you can download your info."

"How did he get in the office?" Amy asked naively.

"We have our ways," he answered.

Ryan looked up at and me and smiled, then turned to Amy. "Amy, Douglas formed a bond with Digger and is asking if he needs to go for another walk."

Amy picked up her little fur-baby. "Yes, I'll get his stuff."

Forty-five minutes later—no Digger, no Doug.

CHAPTER 21

Ryan tried to call Doug's cell phone.
No answer.
He phoned Ted Davis.
No answer.
Marlin Fanning and Bobby Johnson were elsewhere watching Ryan's house and Amy's mom's place. There was no other choice but to call Roger Simon. He said he would send a squad car, and he would be there himself in ten minutes.

We waited.

Ryan paced and Amy worried about Digger. I felt sick, and responsible, just like I had since I realized my actions the night of the fire had probably caused this entire tragedy.

It seemed like forever before we heard sirens. Ryan went down when he was sure the police had arrived. Kline had worked for him for years. Ryan was visibly upset. I snapped my gun on my waist and began walking behind him.

"You should stay up here where you're safe."

"No, you should. This is my fault entirely, and I'm going to put a stop to it."

"That's very noble, but going out into the danger of the night isn't going to solve anything."

I didn't bother to say anything else. I put both hands on my hips and gave him my most defiant look.

"Jeez, Kate."

His body language screamed defeat. When he stepped into the elevator, I walked in beside him and called back over my shoulder, "Amy, I'll be back with Digger as soon as I can."

If Amy answered, her retort was lingering on the other side of the closed door.

The street was once again lit up like it was noon instead of midnight. Police cruisers kept pulling up, and neighbors came out of their apartments and houses in droves. What a sight.

Ryan went to talk to Fanning and Robertson who showed up together. He looked over at me and mouthed, "Stay put, please," while they joined the police in the search for Doug and Digger.

Reluctantly, I nodded, but then I heard a noise to my left and was compelled to walk toward it. Digger! His leash was hung up in a big bush. He whimpered and shook.

When I tried to free him, he snapped at me. I talked to him in my best pet voice, but he was having no part of it. I didn't want to leave him alone to go get Amy, so I went to the other side of the bush where I thought he went in and pulled with all my might. He came loose and was so scared, by that time, he jumped into my lap.

I put the loop of his lead over my hand to my wrist and then wrapped it around about three times. The dog was not going to get away from me. A Saint Bernard couldn't get away from me the way I had him tethered.

Something hit me. It wasn't a person. It was a stick, a stick with a point on it. Thank goodness, it went through the fleshy part of my arm and didn't hit anything vital. It struck with such power it knocked me to the ground. The force of the impact sucked all the air from my lungs. My vision faded to nearly black. I struggled to stay conscious and closed my eyes to concentrate. I needed air. I felt someone standing over me. I opened my eyes but couldn't lift my head. There were boots and black-cuffed trousers. I tried to look up but the pain in my arm as I lifted my head sent me into a panic. Whoever it was touched me. I wanted to scream!

I had no air.

I had this feeling once before when I was in the third grade. I had run as fast as I could, jumped for the top rung of the jungle gym, and missed. I hit so hard my lungs were completely empty. I remember thinking I was going to die.

My lungs expanded ever so slightly. As I became more aware, the pain intensified.

"Are you okay?" It was Ryan.

"Yes." It came out as a faint whisper.

"You just couldn't stay put." He tried to sound angry, but it came out as concern.

"Dog." I sounded stronger.

"Was the dog worth getting hurt over?"

I pulled on the lead to make sure Digger was still there. "Yes."

He kissed my cheek and sat beside me. I heard him say into his cell phone, "We need a paramedic over behind the sumac. Same kind of injury, but not as serious."

I wished I could sit up. "What happened?"

"Doug's pinned to a tree with one of those sticks clear through him. He's awake and talking but they're waiting for a doctor because they're not sure whether it will increase his injury to remove it."

"Someone was here," I whispered.

"Obviously." He patted my arm and wiped the sweat off my forehead with his shirt sleeve. "What did he look like?"

"I only saw feet and pant legs. I wanted to look up but I couldn't. The shaft hit me with such force it knocked me to the ground. I lost all my air." The energy I expended to say all of that made me dizzy again.

"Can you describe the boots and pants?" he asked.

"Black suede boots above the ankle, cuffed legs on the trousers."

"Think about it. Did you have the impression it was a fat person or a thin one? Were they woman's boots or men's? Were they woman's slacks or men's trousers?" He fired the questions at me like a professional.

I closed my eyes and tried to picture what I saw earlier. "They were unisex, both the pants and the boots. The kind of boots you see when you're hiking. They had a crepe sole. The cuffs were narrow. I would say the person was thin, and tall."

Two paramedics came racing through the bushes. The first thing they wanted was for me to let go of Digger so they could move my arm. I told Ryan I would let them treat my arm if he promised to take the dog upstairs to Amy immediately.

He said yes, but he was back in an instant so he probably delegated the job to one of his men.

"This isn't bad," the paramedic, whose badge read Logan, told Ryan. "Only a flesh wound. It must have come with a lot of force to go clean through like that." He kept talking. I knew it was to take my mind off the pain as they maneuvered my arm to dislodge the stick. "I heard my dad talk about these kinds of weapons in Viet Nam. He said the Viet Kong would rig up thirty or forty giant slingshots and then have some sort of trigger so when the enemy stepped on a certain spot it would release all of them. Lots of our guys died that way."

"So this is an Asian thing?" I asked.

"Yeah, I guess it is," he replied.

Ryan said nothing. He stroked my other arm and wiped my forehead periodically. I could feel sweat dripping into my eyes, in spite of his best efforts. It felt like hours passed before the stick came out of my arm. It missed the bone but it looked like someone took a big bite. Once it was free, the pressure let up and I felt better.

"You need to go to the hospital and get checked out. There might be some bark in the wound. We're going to apply a pressure bandage so this thing won't bleed, but it won't hold for long, so don't think you can skip going in. Or we can take you now, with us?" The medic sounded serious.

"No," Ryan said. "We'll bring her over as soon as I'm sure my man is okay.

"Yeah, that's pretty horrible." From the look on his face, I didn't think he meant to say that.

Ryan nodded and helped me up. We stood quietly while the EMTs added a sling to my outfit. Then we walked toward all noise, and Doug.

Doug was pasty white. He had lost a lot of blood. I could tell he was conscious. His eyes were closed and his breath hardly noticeable.

Ryan stepped up next to him. "Hey, buddy. I called Teresa and told her you got hurt and to meet us at the hospital in an hour. I didn't think she needed to come here."

Doug opened his eyes and tried to smile. "Thanks."

"The dog's safe and sound and upstairs with Amy, so stop worrying about it."

Doug closed his eyes again.

Ryan walked over to where the doctor, a nurse, and two paramedics were discussing what to do. I sat on a park bench about ten feet away and leaned back. Now was not the time for me to require anyone's attention. I would stay close, so they wouldn't worry, and stay still so I didn't hurt so bad.

Someone sat beside me. It was Amy. "How are you?"

"Fine. You should be upstairs with Digger. You don't need to tear your stitches."

"I'm good. Digger's asleep on the middle of my bed. He ate and settled right in. I don't think he realizes I'm not there. Thanks for finding him. He's been my best friend for almost twelve years. He knows all of my darkest secrets and loves me anyway."

"Sometimes I think I need a dog. I'm fond of mini dachshunds. Maybe when all this is over." But I knew it was unlikely.

"Listen, when Davis brought the dog back, he told me what happened. Those *impalers*, as they're called, are an ancient oriental weapon. Things keep pointing to our Mr. Woo-Wu. As soon as possible, we need to get on this so we can find Lizzy. I was thinking today. We stopped getting texts from her. It's not a good sign," she said.

I reached into my pocket and brought out a phone. "I haven't even turned on this cell Ryan got me. Have you?"

"Yes, that's what I was doing while I was waiting for the two of you to come back. It's an awesome phone, compared to what I had." Leave it to Amy to find something good in any situation

I turned on the phone. "Ryan likes the best.

We heard a scream that I'd swear they heard in Illinois. It came from Doug. They used a chainsaw to cut the impaler as close to his chest as they could. Then they leaned him forward and used a handsaw to release him from the tree. He went into cardiac arrest and, for the next twenty minutes, they tried to get him back.

Ryan paced and watched, paced and watched. We heard someone say, "We have him back. Let's get him to the mother ship while he's stable."

People began to scurry around, picking up equipment, carrying Doug to the ambulance, and, within a minute, they were all gone. Ryan walked over to us.

"Shouldn't you go with him?" I knew he wanted to.

He raised his foot and rested it on the edge of the bench. "I want to but I want you safe also. Looks like bodyguards and dog walkers are not enough."

"Davis is here. We can go back up to the apartment, which is completely safe, and you go be with Doug," I suggested, trying to sound reassuring.

"What about your arm?" he asked.

I turned to look at the huge wrapping on the upper part of my arm. "It isn't bleeding and I swear I won't move it. We can go have it cleaned out once we know your friend is okay."

"He *is* my friend, you know? He works for me, but we go back a long way. I was best man at his wedding," Ryan said, mostly to himself.

"I didn't realize he was married." Of course, I had never asked.

"Yes, his wife is Teresa. I called her. She's on her way to the hospital."

"I swear, Ryan, we'll be fine. Take us up, you and Davis. Check things out and then go. We promise not to buzz anyone up, and they can't get in otherwise," Amy told him.

He was already helping me up. "If you're sure?"

"We're sure," I said sincerely.

Amy nodded in agreement.

Davis and Ryan looked over the entire apartment, including the closets and under the beds. They locked the balcony doors and pulled every drape in the place. When they were satisfied we were okay and the apartment was secure, Ryan handed me my service weapon and Amy a nine millimeter he had brought up with him. "I am going to take an elevator key. Don't go out, don't let anyone in. I'll be back as soon as I can. No one is outside to keep an eye on you. Fanning and Johns are on their way to the hospital. It will take me a couple of hours to find someone, since it's the middle of the night."

"We don't need anyone. Go. We're fine."

He kissed me lightly on lips and smiled at Amy. "Okay. This time, stay put."

"I swear," I said.

The clock flashed two-thirty-seven.

CHAPTER 22

When I awoke, it was dark and still. The clock on my dresser let me know it was ten -thirty-six a.m. I had my clothes on, laying in my own bed, on top of the covers with my gun resting near my right shoulder. After a trip to the bathroom, I tiptoed toward the living room. Amy was up watching TV, but she had the sound muted.

"Practicing lip reading?" I asked.

"Oh, hi, I didn't want to wake you. Since Ryan hasn't come back, I took a piece of newspaper out on the balcony and let Digger do his business on it."

"Good idea," I said. "I need to set my phone up so I can see what is going on in the world. I didn't realize how much I relied on it."

Amy handed me my phone. "I already did it for you. Since I did mine first, yours was easy.

"Thanks. I don't feel good about Ryan not coming back," I said.

Amy shut off the TV. "Me either."

I called. He didn't have to tell me what happened. I could hear it in his voice. Doug died about five a.m. from loss of blood and some sort of poison that got into his body when the shaft went through his spleen and sliced the edge of his liver.

Doug's wife Teresa was with him when he died, and so was Ryan.

"I have four new men coming to guard you." The grief in his voice was disheartening. "They're going to bring you to the hospital to get that wound looked at. The doctor told me that sometimes they can't stitch it if you wait too long. The four men are Terry Wallace, Danny Joyce, Nathan Wilcox, and Benny Boyd. They're well trained and loyal. When they ring the bell, you'll ask them what they had for breakfast. If they don't each give you the proper answers, don't let them in. Do you need to write them down?" He obviously wasn't taking any chances.

"No, well, maybe. Amy, hand me that pen. Okay, I'm ready."

"Terry will say an omelet; Danny, avocado; Nathan, a ham sandwich; and Benny a bagel. Got it?" he asked.

"Yes," I answered.

Before I could say anything else, he said, "Okay, I have to go. I'll check in when I can."

I felt like crying. "Ryan, I am so sorry."

"I know. Who would have thought?"

I could picture him shaking his head in disgust and couldn't hold back the tears. Amy came over to the couch. Through my sobs, I told her what Ryan said. Another life lost, and it could be my fault. The thing to do was go outside, stand in the middle of the road, and let them have me. At least no other innocent person would die.

When I said as much to Amy, she said if I made a step toward the elevator, she would call Ryan. The last thing he needed was to have to worry about me when he had just lost his friend.

I unlocked the door and went out on the balcony. If they wanted to shoot me, let them. The fresh, crisp, cool air did wonders. I realized it was the first real deep breath I had taken since I got the wind knocked out of me. It felt glorious, most of my morose mood lifted. I had a renewed determination to find out who was trying to ruin our lives.

I sat on the floor with my feet out in front of me and took another cleansing breath. "Amy. Come out here."

"Oh my, it feels good out here," she said with a smile.

I patted the space next to me, signaling for her to sit. "Doesn't it, though?"

"We need to get to the bottom of this—now," she said.

I leaned back on the wall behind me. "I agree. What do you suggest?"

"I suggest we find out everything we can about Jasmine Wu and her father, Stanley Wu."

"Are you sure he's her father?" I asked.

Amy scooted back until she was propped up against the open door. "Yes. And something happened to make him start killing my friends and your family. I want to know what it was. Is she dead or maimed or is he just crazy? What is it?"

"Okay, let's get a background check on both of them. We can do that without leaving here." I intended to keep my promise to Ryan and stay in the apartment.

I could hear my cell phone ringing in the other room, but with my arm I couldn't get up fast enough to answer it before it stopped. Ryan had left a message, wondering if his men had arrived. Strangely, they had not.

The buzzer went off, and Amy and I scrambled toward the intercom. The bodyguards had arrived. They had food, drinks, and the proper passwords, so we rang them up.

The guys were pretty much what I expected. They were well mannered, impeccably groomed, and ready to help in any way they could, starting with taking Digger outside for a walk. This time, three of them went and one stayed with us.

While he waited for his co-workers, he put the groceries on the table, checked the windows, as if he thought someone could get in, and gave me a look when he saw the balcony door open.

Calmly I walked over and closed it.

Within fifteen minutes, Digger was back, and they were gone. Bobby gave me his phone number and they assured us they would be outside if we needed them. Amy and I decided to see what kind of food they left us before we went back to work. Since I'd been five years old, my stomach had always gotten in the way of my determination. I could tell that Ryan had made the grocery list. They brought French vanilla latte for the Keurig, blueberry bagels, cream cheese, spiral cut ham, Jewish rye bread, and Oreo cookies. My heart melted a little, knowing that, with all he had to do, he was thoughtful enough to see that Amy and I had food we liked to munch on.

Thirty minutes later, with my stomach full and my determination back on track, we were finding out all sorts of things about the Wus.

Stanley Wu was second generation American. He served in Viet Nam, so he would know about *impalers* and other sorts of Asian weapons. His grandfather started Wu Enterprises after coming to America in 1913. His father took over in 1948, and then Stanley took the reins in the 1970s. He was sixty-six years old.

He had no criminal history. His business was number one of the top forty importers in the US and a premier importer of high priced Chinese art. He even had a Chinese government clearance to appraise Chinese artifacts.

Listed among his accomplishments was father of Jasmine Wu, US Olympic skier.

Next, we worked on getting to know Jasmine. She went to private schools in St. Louis, graduated first in her high school class, and Magna Cum Laude from Fonnebonne University with a degree in Sports Management and a minor in Art.

She qualified for the US ski team when she was fourteen and skied in her first Olympics at age seventeen. She continued to ski until her critical injury in the Jump Club fire. She lost both legs at the age of twenty-six.

Jasmine fell back on her second love, art. She attended the Kansas City Art Institute to further her craft. Jasmine Wu's paintings had sold for as much as sixty thousand dollars although none had sold since 2011. She had lived in seclusion since that time.

"Interesting, don't you think?" Amy loved a mystery.

"Yes, yes, I do. I think we're on the right track."

"I will be glad when we're no longer penned up here so we can move on what we know," she said.

I hated surveillance. "I'd bet my last dollar that Stanley Wu is behind all of this."

"So would I," Amy agreed.

The intercom sounded and Ryan's voice squeaked on the other end. "I'm coming up, don't shoot."

We both grinned.

Ryan looked gorgeous and exhausted. He had on a gray cashmere jacket, tan chino pants, and a shirt that was a color I couldn't begin to put a name to. It was somewhere between gray and tan, and yet that was impossible.

I couldn't help myself. I walked over—me still in my fuzzy robe—and hugged him. He didn't seem to mind how I was dressed.

"You don't know how good it is to see you," he said. "I came to take you to the hospital to have that arm looked at. We need to get you fixed up and find out who is behind all of this. I'm not prepared to lose anyone else, and whoever it is seems determined to do us more harm."

"Can you give us a few minutes to get dressed? I'm sure Amy doesn't want to stay here."

Amy stood. "*No*, I want to go with you."

"Okay, ladies, get ready. Is there any more of that latte around here?"

"On the counter," Amy answered.

She went her way and I went mine. There was no way I could shower with my arm. I washed up the best I could and put on some loose comfortable slacks and a matching sweater. I dressed it up with earrings and a scarf. I stood back and surveyed myself in the mirror. I would pass. My hair was a mass of curls that I could control with product but today they would have to stay an unruly mess. I grabbed a scrunchy so I could have Amy put it up off my neck for me. There was no way my arm was going up so I could do it.

When I got back to the front room, Ryan lay relaxing on the couch with his sweet coffee, reading the reports we'd generated on the Wus. "Wow, you gals have been busy. This is very helpful." He handed back the papers. "After I go to the funeral home with Teresa tomorrow, I think we should go pay this man a visit."

"We agree," Amy said.

"Okay then, let's get this over with." I held up the ponytail holder. Amy knew what I wanted and took care of my hair.

We were at the hospital for about two hours. Ryan's men were everywhere. They paced, guarded, and scrutinized everything and everybody. I found it unnerving. I knew it was necessary, but we sure were conspicuous.

Due to the miracles of modern medicine, I didn't need stitches.. Because of the poison they found in Doug, I had several blood tests. They found nothing but cleaned the wound with some new kind of antiseptic anyway. The doctor put something he called *second skin* on my arm. First, they took what looked like super glue and put it on both open edges of the wound like you would to pieces of broken glass and held it together a little at a time until it was closed tightly. After about fifteen minutes, he took a can of something and sprayed it over the glued area, waited another five minutes. He repeated this three times and said. "You don't have to give this arm any special treatment. You can shower, swim, or do anything you want. In about two weeks, this outer bandage will begin to disintegrate. About a week after that, it should be as good as new. You have a lot of soft tissue damage so move your arm as much as possible. The nurse will be in with some papers for you to sign and then you're free to go."

"Thanks, Doctor," we all said at once.

The day faded away while we were in the emergency room. We didn't finish until after four. Ryan needed to go to Doug's house and pick up Teresa. Her mom and dad were coming in from Denver and, after that, he felt he should take a backseat in the preparations. Of course, he assured her that she would be taken care of and so would their two children, Doug Jr., age fifteen, and Ella, age eleven.

I felt even more horrible than before. Was this all my fault? I couldn't shake the feeling that it was.

Ryan wanted to feed us. We were not as much hungry, as we were frustrated by being locked up and worried. There hadn't been any word from Lizzy in three days.

Nothing could be done until morning. We went through Steak 'n Shake and loaded up on food to take back to our jail at my apartment. Ryan gave us a list of things to do, which included making an appointment with Stanley Wu and continuing our research on him and Jasmine.

I figured it was busy work, but I was tired and fussy like a three-year-old and sat in the car with my arms crossed, hating myself for the situation I was sure I created.

Ryan walked us to the elevator and rode up with us. When Amy got out, he told her he wanted to talk to me a minute and pushed the button to close the door.

"I could use a hug," he said.

I stepped closer to him and hugged him as tight as I could, buried my face in his shirt, and relaxed as he held me back.

"What have I done?" I asked.

"I'm not sure you did anything. She was penned under that table long before you walked by her. If someone is killing because of it, it's on him or her. Give yourself a break. Things will look better when you get out of this apartment, and we are actually working on the case. That will happen in the morning."

I didn't let go. He gently pushed me away and raised my face to his eyes so he could see me. "Would you care if I came back here tonight? I don't want to go to my place and I don't feel like being alone."

"By all means," I said.

He smiled. "Don't shoot me, okay?"

I smiled back and he kissed me.

For a moment, all was right with the world.

CHAPTER 23

By eight o'clock the next morning, we were all sitting at the dining room table eating bagels with cream cheese and drinking lattes. The mood was festive, in spite of the happenings of the days leading up to it. I knew it was because we were finally going to do something.

Our appointment with Stanley Woo/Wu was at ten. Ryan, Amy, and I ate and chatted about how to handle the meeting. We were on our way by nine. There was a car in front of us with two of Ryan's men and one behind us with two more. I felt like a superstar in a motorcade.

We arrived with ten minutes to spare. One car dropped off at the entrance to the parking lot. The other passed us, went to the far end, turned around, and parked facing us. We put on our best professional faces and went inside.

The place was impressive. To get to the office we took an elevator to the third floor. From the landing, we looked over the vast warehouse with workers pulling product and moving it from place to place. The woman who greeted us was impeccably dressed in a black spring pantsuit with a vivid red figure eight scarf around her neck, red pump heels, and all red accessories. She carried a clipboard where she jotted down our names and repeated them back to us in a deep British accent. After asking if we wanted coffee or water, which we refused, she slipped quietly out of the room.

She was back almost instantly, bidding us to follow her down a long hallway. On both sides hung large framed pictures of the Chinese landscape. I didn't know much about China, but I recognized a tea field, the Great Wall, the Oriental Pearl Tower, and the Lama Temple.

At the end of the hall, she opened the door and ushered us into an office that looked nothing like an office. It was a replica of what I supposed a Chinese aristocrat would live in. Were it not for a desk in front of a massive window at the far end, I would have thought I was in a palace. I stole a look at Amy. I wondered if she had met Mr. Wu in this room. Surely, if she had, it was something she would have shared. I didn't want to sit down and conduct business. I wanted to start at one point and walk completely around the room, looking at all I could see. Instead, I sat with Amy and Ryan on a finely upholstered sofa to the left of the desk.

An older Oriental man came through the same door we had entered and walked up to us. He bowed to Amy and said how nice it was to see her again. He then turned his attention to me and nodded along with the words, "Ah, my pleasure, Mrs. Nash." He then looked at Ryan and innocently remarked that he didn't know who he was. Ryan introduced himself. Then Mr. Wu moved effortlessly to a small table about three feet away and began to pour tea. He didn't ask us if we wanted tea, he just began serving.

"Wong Lo Kat is one of the teas we Chinese are most proud of. Although it is smooth and refreshing, I know Americans sometimes like cream and sugar."

We said we would take it plain. I wondered for a brief moment if he was going to poison us, but he poured four cups, passed three out, and began sipping the fourth one himself.

I took a deep breath. I was almost sure this was the man in the video. The one who argued with Lizzy the day she went missing.

He also fit Amy's description to a tea. He stood about five feet, six inches and looked Chinese but had sandy-blond hair that did not looked dyed. He wore a vivid green running suit, black Nike running shoes, and had a deep tan. If I had to describe him, I would say an average executive, except for the jogging suit.

"Mr. Wu," I began. "My associate—" I nodded toward Amy. "—says you would like to use our detective services because you think someone is stealing from you."

"That's correct." He had no accent whatsoever.

"What do you think is missing?"

"My daughter Jasmine's paintings."

Really? Really, he couldn't come up with anything better than that? I felt Ryan tense beside me.

"Your daughter is the painter, Jasmine Wu, is that right?" I asked.

He nodded toward me. "Yes, how good of you to know that."

Oh, he was good. He knew we knew who she was. He was a great actor.

"I haven't seen any of Jasmine's work lately. I have always been a fan. Has she stopped painting?" Amy asked.

He looked off into the distance, as if he were in pain, but when he looked back, his eyes revealed nothing. "No, it has been sometime since Jasmine has painted. She was in a terrible accident some years ago, and I'm afraid it has taken its toll on her. She took up painting after her skiing career was destroyed by her accident. I thought she was quite good, at both painting and skiing," he said in a whisper of a voice.

Ryan took up the slack. "So when did you begin noticing her paintings were missing?"

"About ten days ago," he answered.

Right when Lizzy went missing, I thought. "How many are gone?"

"Only two, but they were special. She painted them for me after we took a trip to China some years ago. She painted them before she went to art school."

"Didn't your daughter attend Kansas City Art Institute?"

"Why, yes, Miss Nash, she did. Now I know why your agency has such a good name. You do your homework. I am impressed."

"Well, Mr. Wu," I said, as I set down my teacup. "A dear friend of mine was an instructor there, and, she was impressed and told me all about her."

He pursed his lips. "Who is your friend?"

I looked him straight in the eyes. "Lizzy Smith."

It was the first time he betrayed himself with any emotion. He eyes clouded, and he glanced toward something in the corner. I couldn't tell what it was. It all happened in an instant and I was hoping Ryan or Amy had been quicker at following his eyes and could tell me what he was looking at.

We spent the next fifteen minutes discussing what we would do and what it would cost him. He pressed a button under the table and miss black-and-red came back into the room. Mr. Wu got up and whispered something to her. She left and came back with a check, which he signed and handed to me. It was for ten thousand dollars. We all shook his hand and his assistant led us back to the elevator.

None of us spoke until we were in the car. Then Ryan said, "From the way he acted, I would say he knows Lizzy."

"I saw him look at something in the northwest corner of the room, but I couldn't tell what it was," I said

"It was one of Lizzy's paintings, and it's signed to Stanley from Lizzy," Amy said.

I looked at Amy. "How do you know that?"

"He wasn't so prompt the other day. I waited in the room for about five minutes. During that time, I looked around. The painting was dated 2005."

"And you didn't think that was important enough to tell us?" Ryan said.

Amy stopped and put her hands on her hips. "Come on, guys. When have we really had time to sit and talk? With car bombs going off and people being impaled, someone dying, and bodyguards everywhere, it doesn't lend itself to remembering much of anything."

"I guess you're right," I said, "but we have time now, so let's talk."

Ryan took out his phone and called Nathan Morris in the car ahead of us. He told them to head for Blues City Deli in Benton Park on McNair Blvd. He said he was tired of hiding and intended to have lunch in the restaurant. Then we followed their car, with the other two men still following us.

It was twelve-thirty when we got to the deli, and it was busy. Amy and I got a table in the sun, yet not near the front window. No use tempting fate. The four men placed themselves strategically.

I saw them split up. One went around back. I guess he was guarding the back door. Nathan stood just inside the front door, one was on the sidewalk, and the last leaned on Ryan's car. I felt like everyone was staring at us, and they were. They were trying to figure out who in the place warranted all the firepower. They were soon off to other conversations, except for a young couple who spoke a few words to one another, left their place in line, and then walked out the front door.

Couldn't say I blamed them for leaving. With the number of people who had been gunned down for no reason in the past few years, they probably didn't want to take a chance on something happening.

Ryan came to the table with a number. He sat between us, and we began discussing things in hushed tones so no one could hear.

"What did you think of Mr. Wu?" Ryan said.

"If I didn't know what I know, I would take his case and think I was making a lot of money for nothing." I took out the check and looked at it again. "Ten thousand dollars is a lot of money for watching a warehouse. Come on, there's only the front door, the loading docks, and the back door. Why didn't he put up cameras? He could do that three or four times for the money he just laid out."

Our conversation stopped while the server put three huge, Italian-roast-beef sandwiches on the table, along with several sides and drinks. "Are those men with you?" he said, nodding toward the door.

"Yes, yes, they are," Ryan said. "I'm sorry, it can't be helped. Miss Arnie here is a visiting diplomat, and her safety is a top priority."

The server glanced toward me and I gave him a coy smile.

"Do you care if I let that float around in here? The patrons are nervous, and we don't want to lose any more business."

"Sure," Ryan said. "Be discreet. Don't announce it on the PA. We'll finish our lunch and be on our way."

The waiter began to back away. "Oh, no, sir, take your time. Enjoy."

Ryan gave him his biggest grin. All Amy and I could do was sit with our mouths open and hope no one asked for an autograph.

We had no time to respond to what had happened. Ryan's cell phone rang and he answered. "When?" he asked. "Okay, we'll be there in about an hour. No use hurrying if she's gone." He put his phone away slowly, as if he were taking extra time to think. "Someone was at Lizzy's apartment about three this morning. Jeremy thinks it was a woman dressed as a man. He thinks that because the person was tall and slight, and didn't move like a man. Anyway, he watched whoever it was walk straight up to the front door and use a key to unlock it.

"They were there for about a half hour. He didn't want to move away long enough to call me. Whoever it was, left with a suitcase and headed north. He had no trouble following and tailed her until she got into a dark blue Mercedes with no license plates. His car was a mile or so back.

He jogged back and then went to the place where the person got into the car. He spent all this time trying to find the car, but couldn't."

Amy put her sandwich down. "Was the person a passenger in the car, or did they drive it away?"

"Whoever it was, was the driver," Ryan answered.

We finished our lunch in silence. I was sure we each had a million thoughts in our heads. Could it have been Lizzy? When we were about finished with lunch, the same waiter came over with a large sack of food that I assumed Ryan bought for his men. He left an enormous tip, and we left.

Amy and I stood quietly while Ryan talked to Nathan about what happened at Lizzy's apartment. They spoke for about two or three minutes, then Ryan handed him the bag of food, and we walked over to the car where one of the guys stood. "No one came near the car, sir," he said. "It's perfectly safe."

We got in and drove to University City to Lizzy's apartment.

Now what? It was the only thought I had.

It was a silent ride.

CHAPTER 24

The first car was there when we arrived. They were walking around the place, checking windows and the front door. I was hoping I could discern what was missing when I got inside.

I found out a minute later that it would not be so easy. The place had been ransacked. My stomach rose to my throat, and I thought my lunch was coming back up, but it didn't.

Everything in the place was flung on the floors, every drawer was tossed. The mattresses were on the floor, there was paint thrown on the painting Lizzy had been working on when she went missing. It was horrible. I called Roger Simon and he was there in minutes.

"How did you get in?" he asked.

"We've been friends since college," Ryan answered and looked at me. "We both have a key."

Amy was wondering around, looking at things. I noticed she was careful not to touch anything.

"I don't know what to think," Roger said.

I bent down to look at a piece of paper I thought might be important. "Me either."

"Where's your man who saw the suspect?" Roger looked around for someone besides us.

"I hope he's in bed. This happened in the middle of the night. He's been trying to find the car. I didn't find out about all of this until almost one. I'll send him to the station to give a statement after he's rested." Ryan was firm.

"Sounds good. I'll send a forensic crew over, and we'll see what we can find."

"Thanks." The two men shook hands and we left.

"What do you think?" I asked Ryan and Amy when we got into the car.

"I think it's a smoke screen," Amy said. "Whoever it was went to that apartment for a specific reason. They did all of that to cover up what they were really doing."

"We didn't have a chance to look around like you did," I mused. "What makes you think that?"

Amy was in the back seat. She leaned forward to answer. "For one thing, she's a painter and there were no paint brushes."

"They *were* there before," I stated.

"And the clothes in the drawers were not gone thru. Some of them looked untouched, only taken out where they were. Her hanging clothes were laying on the floor in a neat pile, one on top of the other. If I had to guess, I would say Lizzy Smith needed some things and went home to get them," Amy said, matter-of-factly.

"That's impossible!" Ryan and I said at nearly the same time.

"Is it? How well do you know Lizzy? How much time did you really spend with her? Does she have a gym membership, what's her favorite restaurant, is she dating anyone, what does she do all day?" Amy was, once again, proving she was the consummate detective.

I leaned back hard on the car seat. How many of those questions could I answer?

I heard Ryan take a deep breath. "When you put it that way," he said, "I guess I don't know her well at all."

By then we were back at the apartment. Amy went to her room and I went to mine. Ryan followed me in. "How well do you know Lizzy?" he asked. "Ever had a girl talk where she let go of any secrets about herself? Ever since Amy asked about her specifically, I realize, I know nothing."

I plopped down on the bed. "Lizzy and I were never close. She tried to be a friend when Michael died. She brought food and sent thank you cards for me. She spent the better part of a week just hanging around trying to help. What about you?"

Ryan stood facing me. "When I think about it, I guess I don't know her either. We went to dinner on a regular basis and talked about art and music. If she dated, she never did say. Her quiet reserved good manners, incredible good looks, and talent for small talk made her the perfect companion when I needed someone to take to the opera or a fundraiser. But when I really think about it, I don't actually know anything about her."

"Okay, let's review." I looked up and Amy was standing in the doorway. "Come in," I said.

She sat in a chair on the other side of the room near the balcony door.

I cleared my throat. "I got a text from Lizzy ten days ago saying she needed to talk to me at the gardens behind your house. I went and waited a couple of hours but she didn't show up. I went to her apartment but she wasn't there. You and I—" I nodded at Ryan."—canvassed around the art gallery downtown, her apartment, and the U City loop. We found out she had an argument with who we now know was Stanley Wu. She texted us two more times, once on day three and again on day five and gave hints that she was okay. We have not heard anything for five days. Now her apartment has been ransacked and things are missing. Things like paintbrushes, and we think some of her clothes. Someone who could be Lizzy took them—or not. Stanley Wu has a signed painting of hers prominently displayed in his office. What does all of this tell us?"

"Absolutely nothing," Amy said.

"I agree," Ryan stated. "I think the answer lies with our Mr. Wu. Let's all get some rest. Tonight, we'll be spending the night at the warehouse. I'm going down to let the men go home until eleven p.m. That gives us several hours to rest before a long night. You two okay with that?"

We said we were.

~ ~ ~

The men took Digger out before they left. Amy and the dog went to bed in her room, and Ryan came in with me. He slipped off his shoes and lay on the far edge of the bed away from me. He looked exhausted.

I did the same. I didn't think I could sleep but I did. Within a couple of minutes, I heard Ryan's breathing change, and I didn't remember anything after that.

We got up when the alarm went off at eight. We all showered and changed into dark clothing. I didn't like surveillance. I didn't think anyone did. It was cold, boring, and dangerous. Amy and I made sandwiches and snacks for, what we assumed, would be a long night. Ryan called three of his men and gave them instructions. They were to meet us at the apartment at ten. Seemed like the six of us would all be watching the warehouse tonight.

It was a long and boring night, just as I expected. I, personally, thought Mr. Wu was trying to play us. I didn't know why, but the equation didn't make sense unless he was in the middle of it. We stayed until daylight and then headed for the nearest Starbucks for some coffee.

Under normal circumstances, I was a creature of habit. I had my coffee, bagel, and cream cheese every morning. Then I made a stop by the newsstand. There were only one or two in St. Louis. After that I went to the office where, I worked until five or six, and then to the grocery store and home. If someone wanted to kidnap me, it would be an easy catch. Only, lately, so many things had happened that I strayed from the norm. It was exhausting.

Ryan said he had work to do. He promised he would be back by nine and go with us to the warehouse again with his men. I told him I wasn't going to stay in all the time.

I was shocked when he agreed. "Keep your eyes open and let Nathan Morris drive you. I would feel better."

"I need to get dog food and stretch my legs," Amy said. "This is the most sedentary I have been in twenty years."

"Just be careful. I don't think anyone is out to hurt you, and you're probably safe by yourself, but take Bobby with you, anyway. He's good company and a runner."

Ryan left. Amy and I got cleaned up and went our separate ways. It felt good to have a normal day. She wanted clothes and things from her house. I wanted to go to the office. Nathan loaded up the office computer, and off we went.

I didn't realize how popular we were. Four more people wanted to hire us. None of them seemed odd. One had a cat that was poisoned and he wanted to know who did it.

Another man said his daughter of twenty-two had come to St. Louis and met a boy. He wanted us to check the boyfriend out and see if he was who he said he was. There were two women. One was a watch-my-husband-that-scum case and the other was about a missing ring. I couldn't really follow what she was trying to convey. I would have to call her to find out.

I started with the first one and took the case of the poisoned cat. I got all the information and told him we would be there in about an hour. Amy would be at the office by then. The phone rang.

"Kate?"

"Lizzy, is that you?"

"Kate?" she repeated, as though she hadn't heard me. "Kate, I can't do this much longer. I need help." Then the phone went dead.

I sat in stunned silence. I called Ryan, who didn't answer, and Roger, who did. "I just got a call from Lizzy Smith."

"Are you sure?" Roger asked.

"Mostly. She sounded tired and hoarse."

"Did she call on your cell phone so we can track it?"

"No, the office phone. Can you do anything?"

"No, we weren't set up for it. Do you have caller ID?" He sounded frustrated.

I got up to pace. "Yes, but it came in as Anonymous."

"There's nothing I can do. Tell me exactly what she said."

I told him and he said, "Hum. I don't know what to think about that. At least we know she is alive. I wonder how she got to a phone."

"Roger, we need to find her."

"I know, Kate. I'm working on it as an active case. There are just no leads. She vanished one day and there have been no cell phone calls, no credit card charges, and no sightings. All the things we usually use to track someone down are missing."

There wasn't anything else to say, and we hung up when my cell phone rang. It was Ryan. We went over the same information as I had with Roger. He said he was in a meeting and would see me at nine. He sounded depressed.

About ten minutes later, Amy and Digger walked in. They both seemed happier from a long run and different clothes. I went over everything for the third time. Each time I told it, the worse I felt. My friend or at least someone I had known for fifteen years was gone. I mentally renewed my vow to do something.

CHAPTER 25

Amy, Digger, and I went to see Jack Stockman. He was a short, effeminate man with a balding head and a potbelly. When he talked, he made wide sweeping gestures with his arms.

"Thank you so much for coming. Fluffy's in the house. Someone poisoned him."

Amy looked toward the house. "How long ago did it happen?"

He had tears in his eyes. "It was a week yesterday."

Amy looked at me and then back at Mr. Stockman. "You didn't bury Fluffy?"

"No, I kept him for evidence." He said it like it was normal behavior.

"Where, exactly, is Fluffy?" I asked.

"He's in the freezer."

I let out a breath I didn't realize I was holding. "We don't need to see Fluffy. We only need to ask you a couple of questions." He motioned for us to sit at an outdoor table under a tree in the side yard. "Where did you find the cat?"

"He was lying in the flower bed right over there." He began to cry openly.

I made it a point not to look at Amy.

She, meanwhile, put her hand on his and patted it. "I have a dog, Digger, and I know just how you feel. If someone killed him, I would be devastated and angry."

He took a handkerchief from his pocket, unfolded it with a flourish like a waving a flag, and dabbed the corner of his eyes as a woman does when she doesn't want to ruin her makeup.

"Jack, do you get along with your neighbors?" I asked.

"Mostly. This was Mother's house. When she died last year, I moved in. Fluffy was her cat. He was my last living link to my dear mother. He was only nine. He should have lived another seven or eight years. This is tragic." He put his head down on the table and I stole a look at Amy.

She mouthed the words. "Let's help him."

"Well, Jack, we'll take a walk around the neighborhood and see what we can find out."

"Oh, thank you. Thank you." He waved the handkerchief again.

Jack lived in an elegant neighborhood. Professionally done lawns and swimming pools were the norm. Each had a lovely garden, and I guessed a gardener. I didn't see any swing sets or bicycles laying in driveways.

We knocked on the next-door neighbor's door.

A tall thin gentleman answered the door. "May I help you ladies?" he asked.

"We're looking into the death of one of your neighbor's pets."

The man shook his head. "Jack still trying to find out who murdered his mother's cat?"

"Yes, he's quite upset. Do you know who poisoned his cat?" I was determined to take this seriously.

"Yes, we all do, but no one'll tell him for fear he'll shoot them."

"Well, Jack hired us so he can bury this mystery and his cat. He didn't seem violent to me," Amy said.

The neighbor began to close the door. "Then why hasn't he buried the cat? Why does he still cry when you mention it? It's been over a week."

I put my hand on the door to stop it's forward movement. "Do you have any pets, Mr…"

"No, and it's Jones, Troy Jones."

"Well, Mr. Jones," I said. "There's always someone willing to talk. We could canvas this entire neighborhood and eventually we'll run into someone with the kind of personality who wants to talk. You could save us some time and effort."

He looked over me and to his left, right, and then invited us into his house. We all three took a seat in the family room. "Tony Marconi killed the cat. Every day, the cat, Fluffy, who weighed a good twenty pounds, would lay on Tony's prize lilies. It's hard to believe Jack doesn't know Tony killed the cat. They often fought about keeping the cat at home."

"So did this Tony admit to poisoning the cat?"

"Yeah, he said it was an easy fix. In Tony's defense, he lost a major award because when the judges came by, Fluffy was lying in the middle of the garden and had broken the stems of the flowers. Tony was livid."

Amy stood. "Where could we find Mr. Marconi?"

"He lives in the Tudor style house with the circle drive at the north end of the street."

"Thanks for your help."

"You're welcome." He showed us to the door.

As we walked casually to the other end of the street, Amy said, "I have a bad feeling about this. After we confront this guy, are we going to go back and confirm to Jack that his neighbor did indeed kill the cat that he's so attached to he hasn't bothered to bury it a week after it died?"

"I think our man is a little skewed in the mental department, but surely he won't do anything. I can see him calling the police to report a case of animal abuse and cause Mr.

Marconi to have to pay a big fine. I don't think he'll do him any bodily harm."

"For what it is worth, Digger has been my best friend for twelve years. He sleeps with me, listens to all of my problems, and is generally the only one I can trust every minute of every day. It would be difficult for me to *not* hurt someone if they poisoned Digger, heaven forbid."

We went back to the car so she could check on the dog. I didn't have any pets, always wanted a cat, but never managed to take the time to get one. Killing someone over a pet sounded a little overboard to me.

Digger was asleep in the backseat. After Amy checked to make sure the windows were cracked so he had enough air and the doors were locked, we resumed our walk to the Marconi house.

When we got there, we paused in awe. It had the most extensive gardens I had ever seen, except on TV or in magazines. He didn't have to mow his lawn. There were lush green plants everywhere. I told Amy I wanted to come back in a month or two and see them in bloom. If I were a cat, this is where I would want to hang out.

We rang the doorbell, and the man who answered didn't look like a gardener. He was at least six feet, four inches and wore a thousand dollar suit and shoes that topped four hundred dollars. I couldn't afford to dress in that class, but I knew quality when I saw it.

"Mr. Marconi?" I decided it probably wasn't him.

"Yes, who are you?"

I handed him a business card.

"Nash Detective Agency?" He handed back the card. "I don't need a detective."

"I'm sure you don't. This is my associate Amy Perkins. We were hired by your neighbor, Jack Stockman, to investigate the death of his cat, Fluffy."

He laughed. "You're kidding me!"

I took a step forward. "No, I'm serious. Do you know anything about the poisoning of the cat?"

"Yes, I think it got poisoned in my garden."

"What do you mean, *you think*?" Amy asked.

"Well, I did drop some antifreeze when I was servicing my car. I have heard cats love antifreeze because it tastes sweet."

I felt my face get hot. "You're telling me you service your own car?"

"Yes, it isn't against the law, you know?"

"I know, but poisoning a cat is animal abuse," Amy said.

I took Amy by the arm and pulled her toward the stairs. "Thanks for your time, Mr. Marconi, you've been a great help."

"Great help? He poisoned that cat." Amy turned around to glare at him as he grinned at her and shut the door.

I had to nearly pull Amy away. "We're going to Jack's house," I said, "tell him what we found out, collect our fee, and be done with this."

"I still say it's the wrong thing to do."

"Amy, what would you have me tell him?"

"We didn't find out anything. We don't need his money if he doesn't like the job we did."

"Where's your faith in mankind? I believe he just wants to know so he can bury the cat and get on with it."

"Are you sure?" she asked.

"Reasonably."

Jack took it well. He said he thought that was the case, but wanted to be sure. He said he needed closure. He handed me a check he already had written, shook both of our hands, and said goodbye.

We were not a block down the street when we heard the gunshots and saw people running toward the Marconi house.

"I guess I was wrong," I said to Amy.

She shook her head. "You had better turn around. Let's see what happened. I told you. If you had a beloved pet, you would have believed me."

"You'll never know how much I wish I'd listened."

All I could think of was Michael, Roomy, Andy murdered, Lizzy missing, and now a stranger, possibly dead because of me. I stopped and closed my eyes. I swore to myself, at that moment, if I saw someone in trouble, even if it was a hangnail, I'd stop and help. Then I made a vow to get a cat and a dog, I'd never had a pet in my life. Maybe it was what I needed to learn empathy. God knows I needed something.

CHAPTER 26

I had been in a reflective mood ever since Jack Stockman shot Tony Marconi. Thank goodness, he was a poor shot and the bullet hit Tony in the left shoulder. Amy and I had to go to Central to give a deposition.

"What possessed me to tell Jack who killed his cat?" the officer taking our statements asked me.

Honestly, all I could do was shrug my shoulders.

We had to hurry through the interview because Ryan called and said there was something on the film taken at the warehouse the night before. He wanted us to come to his house and review it with him. Thank goodness, he'd had the forethought to set up some cameras.

We watched it at least fifty times. It was unbelievable. A tall thin person in a wide-brimmed hat and dark clothes came to the rear door of the warehouse and used what appeared to be a key to get in.

The next ten minutes showed the lights coming on in the northwest corner, where Mr. Wu said Jasmine's paintings were stored.

About twelve minutes into the tape, the person came back out the same door, carrying two large packages. He or she walked straight toward the camera. Dark hair, thin, and face covered with the hat. I took a deep breath. As the person got closer to the camera, I could see the shoes he wore. And the same shoes as the person who stood over me when I was pinned to the tree outside my apartment.

It answered one large question. We knew now it was all connected. I had every confidence we were going to figure it out.

Ryan kept increasing the size of the picture. I kept thinking if it were only a tad bit larger, I could see the face.

Ryan picked up the phone. "I'm going to call my tech and have him come over. He showed me the basics of the system, but I know he can do wonders with this film."

While we waited, each of us came up with what we thought was going on. I started. "The person is too tall to be Stanley Wu. I still think he wanted us at the warehouse so he could keep an eye on us and try once more to kill us. I believe whoever broke in, or actually used a key to get in, works for Wu. We need to dig deeper into the whereabouts of his daughter, Jasmine. One way or the other, I think she's the key."

Amy said she also thought Jasmine was the key to everything. She was having a difficult time talking to me. Digger rested on her lap and she unconsciously stoked his back.

Neither of us told Ryan about the events of the day. If he thought there was something wrong between Amy and me, he didn't say anything.

Ryan shocked us both with his thoughts. "I think the person on the tape is Lizzy."

"It couldn't be!" I said.

"Why not?" Amy and Ryan both said.

"If it was her, why didn't she just walk away? Why not come home?" I couldn't believe it.

"If you remember, the film showed her getting into the passenger side of a Mercedes. Probably the blue one we have seen before. Whoever is driving that car has something on her that makes her stay. Hopefully, Rodney can manipulate the tape so we can see more."

Someone knocked on the door. It was a young man who I guessed was Rodney. He looked like a high school student, but my doctor looked like he was twelve, so I assumed Rodney was older.

After Ryan introduced us, they went over to the desk and hunched over the control panel. Rodney was sitting and Ryan watched over his left shoulder. Within a minute, Ryan called us over. "Play it for them," he said.

In front of us was the surveillance film. It was clear and moving at the pace of one frame at a time. It was impossible to see the face of the thief, but I did know the movement.

Ryan was right.

It was Lizzy Smith. I was sure of it.

We watched to the end of the tape several times.

Lizzy got into the Mercedes. Someone else was driving. Now I was more confused than before.

Rodney showed Ryan how to make the films clear and, within fifteen minutes, he was gone.

"Do you have any kind of scenario to match what we just saw?" I asked.

"Actually, I do," Ryan said. "I think Jasmine Wu's art is worth a lot of money. It went up when she got hurt and, if she's dead, it will go sky high. I think someone's forcing Lizzy to steal the paintings and paint more that can be passed off as Jasmine's. Whoever it is wants to make sure there are plenty of paintings to go around before they announce her death."

"That's a good story." Amy stood and put Digger on the floor. "It would explain why Lizzy went to her apartment and ransacked it to get brushes and other painting supplies."

"I guess we're pretty sure that was Lizzy too," I said.

"Yes, same height, weight, and body language."

I shuddered. "If that's true, then she was standing over me at the apartment."

Ryan turned away from the console. "Could be. I just don't know why."

"It would explain why we can't find her," Amy said. "She's captive somewhere and can only go out with her captor. How she gets a hold of her cell phone once in a while is something I can't explain."

"I don't know what to think," I said.

"While you're thinking, I need to take Digger out. Do you think it's safe?"

"I doubt it. Let me light this place up." Ryan walked toward the door and flipped a switch. The outside lit up like daylight. Amy headed for the door. "We'll all go," he said.

I stood to join them. Maybe some fresh air would clear my muddled brain.

We were out for about ten minutes. Digger was happy and running around as far as the lead would allow. I thought again, I would get a dog. If we took Digger everywhere, we could take my dog too.

I sat on a bench near the back door and tried to make sense of it all. Ryan stayed close to Amy and Digger. His eyes were roaming around the grounds the entire time.

When Digger finished his business, we all went inside.

"I wonder how many blue Mercedes there are in the area," I said.

"They're popular, now that more young people drive them. There was a time not many people could buy a car whose starting price is fifty thousand dollars. Now I see them everywhere." Ryan walked back over to the desk and the surveillance tape. A frame of Lizzy was on the screen.

Amy walked over to join Ryan. "So I wonder if a blue Mercedes is registered to Jasmine or Stanley Wu. Can you pull some strings at Central and find out?"

"Sure, I'll do it now." I reached for my phone. "I can call dispatch."

It wasn't ten minutes until my friend called back, saying neither of the persons of interest drove a blue car, much less a Mercedes. Stanley Wu drove a 2012 Cadillac Escalade.

There was a 2014 conversion van registered to Jasmine, but the tags hadn't been renewed for three years. I guessed the van was equipped with hand controls so Jasmine could drive. I shared my new information with Ryan and Amy and wondered what happened to my detective skills. Not finding out about Jasmine's ride was a rookie mistake.

"Lizzy's vehicle, over in the lot, is a Lexus SUV."

"I wonder if we should look at it ourselves. We would be looking for different things than the police." Ryan replayed the tape. "Look, there's some sort of sticker on the car. I can make out the shape, but not the writing."

We were both hovering now, trying to get a better look at the picture. "It's a figure eight," I said.

Ryan turned his chair around to face us. "What do we know about that shape?"

Amy shook her head. "I don't think it's an eight."

"Why don't you think it's an eight?" I asked.

"It's too fluffy," Amy said.

"I'm not sure what fluffy is, but I see what you mean." I got up to take a closer look at the picture. "Can you enhance that picture like Rodney did?"

"I can try." In a few seconds, the decal was prominent on the screen. It was black, about six inches tall and had a tiny Wiccan symbol in the center of one of the open spaces.

"Did you ever play with a Ouija Board?" Amy grinned. "If the planchette begins to move in a figure eight, it means an evil spirit has control of the board. Considering it has a Wiccan symbol in the center, I would say it has something to do with the Ouija."

I could only stare at her. I didn't go in for such nonsense, yet it made sense because of the evil mentioned in the notes with the murders. Jeez, I hated voodoo, horror movies, Ouija Boards, and anything else that caused me to be afraid.

Ryan didn't say a word. He seemed to be in deep thought. He turned back toward the computer screen and began to move the cursor over the picture of the car as if he was looking for something. "There is it." He put his finger on the picture of the front bumper of the car. He made the picture as large as he could.

"Is that the sign of the devil?" Amy asked.

"No it's a pentacle. It's the most important symbol of a Wiccan. The sign of the devil is close, but not the same. It's from the Wiccan Rede, a poem, handed down for centuries. They honor both God and the Goddess of Wiccan. They record their spiritual journey in the Book of Shadows. They don't use black magic. They are actually a religion of fertility."

Amy and I shook our heads. "How do you know that?" I asked. "Are you a Warlock?"

"The men aren't warlocks. They're called Wiccan. They believe it's best to keep the genders equal."

"Again, how do you know all of this?" I asked again.

"Because about six years ago, Lizzy decided she wanted to be a Wiccan. She wanted to have a baby and couldn't get pregnant."

Amy sat down. "Was Lizzy seeing someone?"

Ryan didn't look at either of us. "No, she wanted a baby, though. She asked me to sleep with her and be the sperm donor."

"Did you?" The thought bothered me.

He stared deep into my eyes and, without blinking, he said, "No. I told her I was saving myself. When I have children, it'll be because I love their mother. Lizzy also made it clear; she didn't want an emotional attachment between me and the baby. She only wanted my sperm."

I sighed. "I'm beginning to think I didn't know Lizzy at all. She and I lived in the same room in college, and she was private then. We laughed, talked, cried together, but we never had a serious discussion about anything."

"I don't think I knew her either. But I bet Lizzy owns that Mercedes and the eight with the Wiccan sign is a Wiccan tribe or whatever you call them."

"A coven, you call them a coven," Amy said.

Ryan nodded. "Well, it's getting late. In the morning, we need to track down the group represented by that decal."

"We agree," I said for Amy and myself.

"I'm a little spooked now. Do you mind if I come back to the apartment with you?"

"No," I smiled at him. I don't think he was nearly as upset as I was. The hair stood up on the back of my neck. If it were only Amy and me home, I didn't think I would be able to sleep.

Amy seemed to perk up some when she found out we would not be alone.

All the way home, up the elevator, and while we checked the apartment for intruders, I held my breath, waiting for the other shoe to fall.

CHAPTER 27

Amy came out of her bedroom. "I would like to go home."

"Now?" Ryan looked at his watch. "It's only nine. If you want to go, I'll have two of the men go with you and one stand guard outside your house."

"I hate to be so much trouble, but I haven't been there for days, and I'm homesick."

"Really, Amy, it isn't a problem. Get your things together, and I'll call Nathan and Bobby. I don't want you to go alone, and I want to make sure no one has been there and it's safe."

"Thanks, Ryan."

She walked back into her room.

I followed and plopped myself on the bed. "Are you uncomfortable because he's here?" I asked, nodding my head toward the door.

"No, you know what a homebody I am. I'd like to soak in the bathtub for a while and let Digger go out in his own yard without a lead. You understand the simple things you miss about home."

"I do understand. You've been super since this all started. You never mention your injuries. Are they healing?"

"I don't mention them because they don't hurt. I can shower and move just fine. I think we were lucky there. Actually, we've been lucky throughout the entire ordeal. Except for Doug. That was horrible. Do you think Lizzy's involved in the killings?"

"No. No, I don't. Someone's controlling her. I feel it. Lizzy has always been a pacifist. I think the key to this entire nightmare is Stanley Wu and his daughter Jasmine. I wonder if Ryan's idea is spot on. I'm determined to find out."

All the time we were talking, she was packing. "Should I strip the bed?"

"No, Mrs. Riley comes once a week. I haven't had her here for her own safety. She's due here tomorrow. Ryan'll probably want to search her."

We both chuckled.

Amy had two bags and I helped her carry them to the elevator. Nathan was there when the door opened and, in less than five minutes, they were gone. I felt a twinge of anxiety when Amy left. I took a deep breath and told myself to let go of stress and worry. It felt so good, I did it several more times.

"I'm starving," Ryan said.

"Me too. Let's see what we have." We raided the refrigerator and fashioned a makeshift meal of pasta, with red sauce, a small salad and a glass of wine. "Tell me some more about Lizzy. I didn't realize you too were so close."

"We were for a while about six years ago. You, Roomy, and Andy all got married within a year and a half of each other. Lizzy and I were both in all the weddings so we went together. It was nothing romantic."

"She asked you to father her baby?"

"There was nothing romantic about that. We had a long talk about marriage. Most everyone, but you, knew how I felt about you and when you got married, I got lots of 'I'm sorry.'"

I picked up my wine glass. "I had no idea back then."

He stayed close. "I know. I'm over having my feelings hurt." He stood, walked around the table, and kissed me lightly. "I was surprised you fell for anyone back then. You were always intense. You wanted to save the world. I figured you would go into politics or the CIA. I was shocked when you picked the police academy."

"I loved being a cop, but I couldn't do it anymore after Michael." I looked down and moved my fork mindlessly around my plate. I was incredibly sad and guilty. I looked at him again. "Homicide is no place for a woman with a murdered husband. I spent all my time worrying about how the loved ones were holding up. I couldn't focus on the job anymore."

He took a step back. "You were devastated, with reason. I swore to myself I would stand by you, no matter what. My feelings for you came rushing back, but I have kept them in check until now."

"I would think you would hate me for using you to ease my pain, on the two occasions I did." I felt like I was selfish about everything in my life.

"It was hard not to let go and smother you but I knew what you were doing, and there's no need to apologize. We got through it." We finished our wine in silence. Ryan helped me clean the dishes up and wipe down the counters. He poured us another glass of wine. "I need to tell you something." He adjusted himself so he was looking at me. "I was happy for you and Michael."

I smiled at him. "I never thought anything else."

"I feel guilty for my feelings, even though I know it's silly. I waited nearly three years to ask you out and you only went because you didn't know about my feelings."

After sitting my glass on the coffee table, I leaned over and put my fingers on his chest. "I have no idea what's going to happen between us. Right now, I feel safe, warm, and loved. We need to get through this Lizzy Smith thing and see how we function in the real world."

"I'm in no hurry. My feelings for you only grow stronger. Being pushy isn't my style."

I moved closer to him with my hand still between us. He hugged me and made a contented sigh.

Quietly, I said, "Was Lizzy seeing someone and she couldn't get pregnant by him?"

He begrudgingly pushed me away. "Back to the case, huh?"

"Yes, I need resolution."

"Amen to that. I hadn't seen her in a while. I was in Germany on company business for several months. It was during your and Michael's first year of marriage, so I don't think you would have missed me. We went to Tony's and half way through dinner, she said she had a proposition for me.

"The proposal was that we sleep together so she could have a baby. She was interested in my sperm and only my sperm. As I told you before, the idea was not appealing to me. I have never been one to sow my seed for only pleasure. It was difficult to turn her down. She's my friend, and a beautiful woman.

"She wasn't sure why I declined, so she offered me the option of leaving my sperm at her doctor's office and he would impregnate her. I explained how I felt. It was tense between us for some months and then she never mentioned it again. Often times, when I saw her, I looked closely to see if she was pregnant, but there was never any sign."

I stood and walked over to look out at the sky. "The way Lizzy jet-sets around the world with her paintings, having showings in several countries a year, it surprises me."

"Me too. I can tell you one thing. I don't think Lizzy is involved in the murders. She's caught up in this somehow, but I don't know for sure why. I still believe it involves money, Jasmine Wu, and Stanley. I turned the everyday running of my companies over to Jason Davidson, my VP. I intend to spend every minute getting to the bottom of this.

Now, it's more important than ever." He smiled at me, took my hand, and ushered me into the bedroom.

I went to take a shower. Ryan opened the balcony door and stepped out. When I returned, he was in bed, asleep. The blanket came to his waist, exposing his bare torso. I watched the rise and fall of his chest and slipped in beside him. I lay close, but not close enough to wake him. Before I fell asleep, he rolled over toward me. He was completely naked.

Far into the night, I worried and fretted about Lizzy, Michael, Roomy, and Andy. I knew I was to blame for them not being here. I fell asleep with the certainly that Jasmine and her father held the key to everything.

I woke early and went into the living room at five a.m.

When Ryan came into the living room at seven-thirty, I had news for him. "Hi, want some coffee?"

"I'll get it. You look busy. What are you working on?"

"The Figure Eight Wiccan Coven—it's in Belleville, Illinois. I've been on their website. Wiccan's aren't anything like I thought they were. Did you know it's a spiritual journey and they probably don't use Ouija Boards?"

"Lizzy filled me in. She joined because a test showed she was infertile. They are all about fertility."

"Their next meeting's tonight at six. I'd like to go and see what information we can get from them."

He came back with coffee in his hand. "Sounds like a good idea."

"By the way, this was in my jacket pocket. It's the coat I had on the night I was impaled with the stick." I handed it to him.

We all have people who make us happy. The love of my life is gone, and you will pay. Evil begets evil.

"It's not a fortune-cookie fortune like the rest of the notes were. It's hand written and poorly at that. We should take it to Roger."

"I agree. This is my to-do list for today." I handed it to him.

"Very ambitious. If we are going to get through this list, I had better shower and put on some clean clothes." He had on a pair of wrinkled jeans and I supposed nothing else.

~ ~ ~

He took the list again when we got in his car. Two new men were there. "How many security men do you have?"

"One hundred-forty-three. I bought a security company from St. Charles the other day."

"Must be nice!"

"It is. Especially now. I have them everywhere. I don't intend to lose anyone else."

I put my hand in his. "Thanks."

"Oh, I believe they will be valuable long after we have Stanley Wu in jail." He squeezed my hand. "Okay, first item. Starbucks for latte and bagels then we head to your office."

I looked out the window, lost in my own thoughts, until we got to the coffee shop.

We walked into the office, expecting Amy to be at the front desk. Instead, a monster of a man in a sport coat and tie greeted us. "Hi, boss."

"Hi, Derrick. Where's Miss Perkin?"

"I put her in the inner office. I figured if anyone came through the door who wanted to do her harm, I could better protect her if they didn't see her when they came in."

"Sounds like a good plan to me." Derrick had stood when we came in. He had to be six-six. Ryan winked at me. "Kate, this young man is Derrick Johnstone. Derrick, this is Kate Nash."

The man extended his huge hand for me to shake. After we exchanged pleasantries, we opened the door to the office and joined Amy.

"I guess you met Derrick," she said to me. "No need to be nervous with him around. He treats me like a Ming vase he's been told not to chip."

Ryan chuckled. "Good to know. Maybe he needs a raise. I'm going to leave you two in Derrick's capable hands. I have some errands to run. Enjoy your breakfast, and I'll be back in time to get to the next thing on the list. Say, two hours?"

"Wonderful," I said, and he was gone.

Amy and I went over business. We didn't have anyone wanting us to do anything until a week from Wednesday.

She put Stanley Wu and Jack Stockman's checks in the bank, paid all of our bills, and wrote us each a hefty paycheck for ourselves.

"Jake's flying in tomorrow and staying until Saturday afternoon. I thought since the bills were paid, and you're working with Ryan on Lizzy's case, I would take a couple of days off."

"That would be fine, but I don't think Ryan will want you to go anywhere without a bodyguard. What do you think Jake will say?" I asked.

"I haven't told him anything about all of this. He worries enough, not being here, I didn't want to try to explain over the phone. When he finds out I might be in danger, he won't be okay with it. Besides, I have felt ultra-protected since Derrick showed up at five this morning."

We discussed more business and a multitude of other subjects while we munched on our bagels and sipped our lattes. Things felt almost normal. I should have known it wouldn't last.

CHAPTER 28

Next on my list, Stanley Wu. The drive took thirty minutes. The same secretary ushered us in, offered drinks, and left us to wait.

It took Mr. Wu nearly ten minutes to come in. Ryan spent his time wondering around the massive office. I sat facing the door. Wu's absence made me nervous.

"Well." The voice came from behind me. "Mrs. Nash, did you come to visit me alone?"

Ryan began walking toward us. "No, she didn't."

"Mr. Meade, good to see you again. I take it you have news about the paintings stolen from my warehouse the other night."

"Yes, we do."

Wu sat down at his desk. Ryan took one of the chairs facing it so I got up and took the other chair.

"Well, don't keep me in suspense. Have you found my thief?"

"We think your burglar is Lizzy Smith."

"Preposterous!" he shouted.

He stood up, walked around the desk, and leaned back on it. I wanted to move my chair back. We all had a personal space, and he invaded mine. I glanced at Ryan who seemed to be relaxed.

"Not the response I expected," Ryan said.

"And why is that? Miss Smith has no need to steal. She and my daughter are close friends. If she wanted a painting, Jasmine would give her one."

"Have you seen Jasmine lately," I asked.

"Heavens, no. My daughter and I have been estranged, almost three years now. I have no idea how she is spending her time or with whom. Since Jasmine's accident, she's been difficult. You know about her injuries, don't you, Mrs. Nash?" He leaned over, his nose only inches from my face.

I felt myself flush.

Ryan must have seen my reaction. "I was there, too."

"Why, yes, Ryan Meade, you owned the building where the inferno took place. Small world, isn't it?" He wasn't trying to hide his disdain for either of us. Thank goodness, he moved away from my face when Ryan spoke.

I took a deep breath.

"Although the Meade Trust owned the building, it was leased to White Enterprises," Ryan said. "Shawn White was two years into a five-year lease when the fire occurred. We were not to blame."

"So they told me when I tried to add your name to the lawsuit for Jasmine. Tearing down the building and building a park was a nice touch."

I hoped my nerves didn't betray me. "Of all of the detective agencies in the area, why did you hire me to track down your thief?"

"Curiosity. I have followed your career ever since you left the police department because of the murder of your husband. That *is* why you left, isn't it?"

I didn't answer. He was letting us know he was involved in the murders, at least *I* thought he was. It was bizarre. The hair stood up on the back of my neck.

Ryan stood. "What is it you actually want of us, Mr. Wu? I have known Lizzy Smith for many years, and I assure you, it was her on the tape. She walked up to your warehouse, unlocked the door with a key, and ten minutes later, she walked out with two paintings. She left in a late model blue Mercedes."

"I find this all extremely interesting. I don't believe I will need your services any longer. Did the check I wrote cover your expenses, or will you require more?"

I stood next to Ryan. "No, we can just call it even."

"Oh, Kate, we will never be even." He turned and walked out the rear door.

No one escorted us through the warehouse this time. We walked out alone. Neither of us spoke until we reached the car.

"Don't touch the car." Ryan took out his phone. "Billy, are you close?"

I didn't hear Billy's side of the conversation.

Ryan nodded. "Come over to the warehouse parking lot and scan my car for bombs and recording devices. We'll be waiting."

Within ten minutes, Billy gave Ryan the all clear, but not before handing him a GPS tracker he found attached to the inside of the rear fender.

"Let's get out of here," I said.

"Agreed." Ryan got in the car and started the engine.

"The man hates us," I said. "You don't need to be a genius to see it."

"I am convinced he intends to kill us," Ryan said calmly.

"Ryan, I don't like this. We need to get proof and find out how Lizzy fits into all of this."

"What's next on your list?"

"Well, I wanted to follow Wu, but since Amy took a few days off, I want to go to Belleville to the Wiccan Coven that Lizzy might be part of."

"We can do both." Again, he called some of his men. "Tail Stanley Wu. Use five or six different cars so he won't pick up on it. There's no address for him except for the warehouse. He has to live somewhere. When you find it, give me a call. Someone stay around and keep an eye on him." He hung up. "There, that's done. Do you have any idea where this place is?"

"I have an address."

He pulled over and set the GPS.

The Coven headquarters sat on some acreage outside of the city of Belleville, Illinois. There was a lodge, so we went in. "Hi, is this the Figure eight Wiccan Coven?"

"It is. Are you here for the meeting?"

"Actually, no. We need some information."

The woman walked toward us. "Sure, what can I answer for you?"

"Do you know this woman?" I held up my phone and showed her a picture of Lizzy?

"Sure, that's Lizzy, Lizzy Smith."

"Is she here?" I asked.

"Oh my, no. She hasn't been around in years."

"Do you know why she stopped coming?" Ryan asked.

"I do, but I'm not sure I should tell you."

"I'm Kate Nash." I gave her my card. "We're trying to find Lizzy. She's been missing for nearly two weeks. She's an old and dear friend."

"Oh, my! She came here because she wanted to have a baby, and we're all about fertility. Haven't seen her for about three years. We heard her lover died and fertility was no longer an issue."

"Did you ever see him?"

She took another step and leaned on the counter that separated us. "No."

"Do you know his name?"

"No. Lizzy was very private about her personal life. She talked about her work, but not much else."

"Thanks for the information. If you happen to see Lizzy, please call me."

We were almost out the door when she said, "I don't think you know Lizzy as well as you think."

I stopped. "What do you mean by that?"

"Sorry, not my story to tell."

What a day!

On the way home, we stopped at Pitcher's Sports Bar and Pizzeria. The food came to us hot and fresh. We ate pulled pork sandwiches, coleslaw, baked beans, and drank beer. The noise level ranked up there with a rock concert. The Cardinals were on TV and every time they scored, the crowd went crazy.

I didn't want to talk so the noise didn't bother me. I wanted to curl up in a big ball and sleep for days, but since I knew that wasn't possible, just being alone with my thoughts would have to do.

One of the men stayed with the car and two more were in the club having a beer at the bar. Bodyguards, Wiccans, GPS trackers, the entire thing weighed on me.

Ryan seemed to notice my mood. On the way to the car, he stopped and hugged me. "It's all going to work out. We'll find out what's going on with Lizzy, we'll stop that psychopath, Wu, and get to the bottom of this."

"Okay, if you say so." I walked around to my side of the truck. Ryan followed and opened the door. That's when I saw it, a piece of paper lying neatly folded on the seat. Ryan reached for it. I grabbed his hand. "It's time we began running this like a police investigation. Don't touch that in case it has finger prints on it. Send one of the guys inside to get a to-go box. We'll put it in there and take it straight to Rodger."

"Sounds like a good idea, but we're not sure what it is."

"I'm pretty sure it refers to me and evil and retribution." He put his hand on my shoulder. "I'm all right," I said. "I'm just tired and frustrated with the case and myself. Someone's trying to kill me and those closest to me. It's time to put an end to all of it."

"You're beginning to sound like the old Kate. I like it, to a point. Not so much as to send these guys away." He nodded toward his men.

I didn't bother to answer.

One of the bodyguards handed me a to-go box. I took a Kleenex out of my pocket and picked the note up by the corner, using the tissue to avoid smudging anything. After it was in the box, we headed toward downtown St. Louis. Ryan drove. I held the box in my lap, as if it might explode.

Donny Chrisman—a tech from the lab, who I worked with for years—put on gloves, opened the box, and unfolded the note. It read pretty much like I thought it would. *Your family and friends are in peril because of your evil ways and lack of concern. It is too late to make amends. Evil begets evil.*

I looked at Ryan. "Do you think my mom is safe in Florida?"

"It's no trouble to have someone watch her. Let me make a few phone calls. I think I can have someone at her house within ten minutes. Call her and make sure she's okay."

I looked at my watch. "It's almost ten so she might not be up, but I'll try." I walked out in to the hall and dialed her number.

She answered on the second ring. She thought something was wrong, but I told her I missed her and was thinking about her and only wanted to say hi. We talked about five minutes and hung up. She was alone, happy, and safe.

I walked back down the hall toward Ryan. "I took care of it," he said. "She'll have around-the-clock protection until this is resolved."

"Thanks."

Donny called us back to the lab.

"It's as I expected, no finger prints. The paper's regular twenty-pound bond, ninety-two brightness, sold at any office supply store, or Walmart, for that matter. I can tell you someone cut it from a larger sheet of paper, and I think the person who cut it was left handed. The way the edge of the paper was cut indicates whoever cut it held the scissors upside down."

"Stanley Wu is left handed," I said.

"So is Lizzy." Ryan looked at me when he said it.

When we got to the apartment, Ryan came upstairs. "After the note, I think I should stay again tonight."

"No. I need some time alone. Stanley Wu, Lizzy, my mom, Amy, and you. It's all too much. I'd love to be alone."

"Should I take this personally?"

"Ryan, do you think if this wasn't going on that you'd be spending every night at my place and be sleeping naked in my bed?"

He studied me. "Honestly?"

"Yes."

"I think we might have worked up to it. There's nowhere I'd rather be."

"It's another thing I can't deal with right now. Try to understand. The deaths of Michael, Roomy, and Andy, and the disappearance of Lizzy might be my fault entirely." I put my hand on his chest. "You're a dear man. I need you to help me with this, and your men to protect my mom and Amy. I don't need it to cloud my judgment and lead me somewhere I might not be ready to go."

He leaned down and rested his chin on the top of my head. "I was hoping you wouldn't notice. I'll leave a couple of men here to make sure your safe. See you tomorrow."

He kissed the top of my head and turned toward the elevator.

I said nothing else to him, and he didn't turn around when he got into the car to go down to the street.

CHAPTER 29

O nce I was alone, I soaked in a steaming tub, to which I added salts and soap beads. The apartment was quiet for the first time in days. When I got out, I dressed in my most comfortable flannel PJs, fixed a cup of green tea, and went into my room. With my head propped up on pillows and a legal pad in my hand, I began to take notes of times and days of the events leading up to tonight.

When I finished, I had a time line. I started with Michael's death and ended with the car bombing and Doug's murder. Next, I wrote down the things that made me the most uncomfortable, starting with Lizzy's disappearance, the fact that Jasmine Wu hadn't sold a painting in three years, and no credit card charges or a cell phone had been detected in that time. Stanley Wu hated me and openly admitted it. The Wiccan told me I didn't know Lizzy and, somehow, someone put a note in Ryan's truck while it was being watched by his bodyguard.

Maybe Ryan was right. Lizzy's kidnapping connected her to Jasmine's art. Stanley Wu wanted to kill me because I didn't help his daughter at the fire, but mostly, before he got rid of me, he wanted to watch me suffer as he killed my beloved friends, one by one.

I must have fallen asleep. In my dreams, Michael came to me, but when I opened my eyes to talk to him, he stood before me with a bullet hole through his left eye. Roomy stood to his right. Lizzy stood behind them in a black hat and begged me to save her. I woke up in a cold sweat, my hair matted to my head, and a scream stuck in my throat. I looked at the clock. It was four-fifteen.

I spent several hours looking for a puppy on Craigslist. Maybe I was losing my mind.

The phone rang promptly at seven. It was Ryan. "Hi, did you sleep well?"

"No. How about you?"

"No. But I got some interesting news this morning. It seems Stanley Wu doesn't have an address because he lives somewhere in the warehouse. I'm not sure where. The guys said he never left and there were no visible lights. They think there must be an apartment contained somewhere, maybe in a basement."

I got up from my computer. "No kidding. That's interesting."

"There's more. The blue Mercedes with the decals on it belongs to Madison Daily."

"Who's Madison Daily?" I asked

"She owns the land the Figure Eight Wiccan Coven use as a lodge and meeting place."

"The plot thickens." I tried to say it in my best villain voice."

"I think we should talk to Miss Daily and find out about her car." He sounded cheerful.

"I agree. Do you know where to find her?"

"Yes, she's Belleville's premier real estate agent. I'll pick you up in an hour. That'll give me time to get you a bagel and a latte."

"Aren't you sweet?"

"Okay, in an hour then."

After a quick shower, I put on my favorite pair of faded jeans and a pink tee shirt. I put my shoulder holster on, added my forty caliber, and slipped on a blue blazer to hide it.

While I waited for Ryan to arrive, I Googled Madison Daily and read her impressive resume. Not only was she a rich woman but she was tall, blonde, and beautiful. She reminded me of Lizzy.

Ryan buzzed in almost exactly an hour. I went down. He was dressed the same as I was in jeans and a tee shirt. I could tell he had a pistol in a holster at the small of his back, even though he had on a jacket. People walked differently when they had a gun on them. I couldn't explain it, but I always recognized it.

I'd lived in St. Louis most of my life yet until recently had only been to Belleville once, and that was last night. We usually stayed on the Missouri side of the bridge. To do things on the east side complicated everything from taxes to taking a chance on breaking an unfamiliar law.

When I finished my bagel, I said, "Did you call ahead and tell Miss Daily we were coming?"

"No. I thought we would surprise her. She reported her car stolen a little over three years ago. That fits into our timeline. I just don't why the timeline is important."

I took a sip of my latte. "Me either, but we know no one has seen Jasmine for about three years, Michael was murdered three years ago, and now the car. It must all tie together, I just don't know how."

He patted my hand. "I don't either, but we'll find out. Every lead brings us a step closer."

"Just so Lizzy is okay."

"That's what bugs me the most. Why was she at the warehouse and who was in that car with her?"

As we pulled up outside Madison Daily's office, I noticed a blue Mercedes parked on the side of the building. "Look, do you see that?"

"Yes, I do, but it isn't the same car. No stickers and this one is new and has tags on it."

"I see all of that. I think it's weird she had a blue one stolen and bought another one."

"You're assuming it's hers?" he asked.

"Yes, I am. Years of being a cop has helped me learn patterns. Your tastes in automobiles don't change just because yours is stolen."

I was out of the truck before he had a chance to come around to get me. I hated it because I was too short to step down and had to slide out of the seat and onto the running board. Out of the corner of my eye, I saw Ryan's men park about a half block away.

Madison Daily sat at a desk on the south side of the room. She got up when we came in. "May I help you folks with anything?"

I reached into my pocket and handed her a card. She read it. If it surprised her that a private detective wanted to talk to her, she didn't show it. "This is Ryan Meade," I nodded toward Ryan.

She smiled and reached out to shake his hand. "*The* Ryan Meade?"

Ryan shook her hand but didn't say anything.

I, on the other hand, said, "Yes, *The* Ryan Meade!"

He shot me a look I couldn't really read, but I took it as embarrassment.

"Please, sit down." She looked at my card. "Mrs. Nash, Mr. Meade, how may I help you this morning?"

"One of our friends is missing. She was seen a few nights ago in a blue 2011 Mercedes with a couple of identifying stickers on it. After some investigation, we determined it was stolen from you."

"Well, yes, I had a car like that taken about three years ago. It vanished without a trace. The police couldn't find it. Strange for it to show up now."

"Where were you when it was taken?" I asked.

"I own some property on the outskirts of town. It was taken there while I was in a meeting."

"And you say that was three years ago?" Ryan asked.

"Yes. Almost exactly. There have been rumors the car has been seen from time to time. Most of the reports come from Pogue, Granite City, and East St. Louis."

"I'm surprised you bought another just like it." I was testing my theory that preferences don't change much.

"It's my dream car. I couldn't resist. I'm much more careful now. I always lock it."

"So it wasn't locked the night it was stolen?"

"No. I was in a meeting. There were dozens of cars there. I knew everyone there, and it wasn't a place you would stumble upon. Do I know your missing friend?"

"You tell me," Ryan said. "Do you know Lizzy Smith?"

Madison turned pale and sat down. "Why, yes I do, and I read in the paper that she was missing, How horrible."

"How well did you know her?" I felt her reaction was real concern.

"I thought I knew her well. She was friends with another artist friend of mine from high school, Jasmine Wu. I only saw her once after the car went missing, and Jasmine dropped out of sight too."

"What kind of meeting were you attending?"

"Oh, a Wiccan festival. I don't go to everything but some of the rituals resonate with me. I couldn't get pregnant, and this was a fertility gathering, so I joined in."

"Do you know if Lizzy went to any meetings after that night?"

"No, I don't. If it wasn't specifically about fertility, I didn't attend. I knew about the Coven because I lease them the land. It was an old girl scout camp I bought some years ago," she explained.

Ryan crossed his legs. "When's the last time you saw Jasmine Wu."

"I'm not sure, but I don't think she had anything to do with the Coven. If I remember correctly, the connection between Jasmine and Lizzy began as student and teacher and became a friendship. Are they both missing?"

"We really don't know much about Jasmine Wu. We're looking for Lizzy. She is a close personal friend to both of us."

Madison looked at her watch. "I hate to bail on this, but I have to show a property."

Ryan and I both stood. "Not a problem, we were hoping you would know more. Thanks for your time."

"My pleasure." She shook both of our hands. "If you ever need any property on the East side, give me a call." She reached down, picked up a card, and handed it to him.

"By the way," Ryan asked. "Did the Wiccan festival help you?"

She had a twinkle in her eye. "Why, yes, it did. We have a two year old and one on the way."

"That's great!" I said. "Thanks for your time."

Once we were in the car, I couldn't help but raze Ryan about Miss Daily. "Well, *The* Ryan Meade, what did you think of that?"

He laughed and started the truck. "I don't even blink at that stuff anymore. People love money and the fact that I didn't do anything to earn mine doesn't seem to make a difference."

"Ryan." I touched his arm. "You don't give yourself enough credit. You inherited the money at an early age. Look at all you've accomplished."

He looked over at me. "Do you ever wonder how I'd be without the money?"

"I know exactly what you'd be, the same loving, gentle, sweet, generous, kind man you are now."

We drove a few miles in silence, and then he took one hand off the steering wheel and put it on top of mine.

He turned down a country road, instead of getting on Highway 111 and heading toward St. Louis. "This area is known as Pogue. Around here's where our real estate friend said the car was spotted."

"Can we look around a little?"

"Sure. I'm just not sure what we're looking for. Sure would be nice if the Mercedes pulled out in front of us and we could just follow it home," Ryan joked.

"Things don't work out that way, at least not in my world. However, I was thinking. Just how many men do you have at this new company of yours?"

"Several hundred, why?"

"Could you have a few cars drive around this area and see if the Mercedes shows up. We know it's around."

He pulled over and faced me. "Do you know how slim the chances of us ever seeing that car again are?"

"Yes, I do, but I'm at a dead end."

He took out his phone. "So am I. We'll try it."

My phone rang. It was Amy. "Someone just tried to kill me." She was breathless.

"Are you okay? What happened?"

"Jake wanted to go for a run so I went to the grocery store. Derrick waited out front. I got what we needed and, as I walked back to the car, someone in a blue Mercedes came all the way up on the curb to try to run me down. Derrick shot out the back window, but they kept driving. Had it not been for a brick curb I tripped over and fell down a hill, they would have run over me."

"Were you able to see the driver?"

"No, the windows were tinted. I think there was only one person in the car. It all happened so quickly. Kate, be careful. This isn't over, and I'm scared. We're going to try and find Jake before someone decides to hurt him too."

"Amy, I'm so sorry. Stay close to Derrick. We'll be right there."

When I hung up, Ryan was already on the phone with Derrick. He swore Amy was fine and he was going to see she remained that way. After Ryan hung up, he called the security office and arranged for six men in six different cars. They were to park in strategic spots around the Pogue area. He was now determined to find the car.

It was unnecessary. As we pulled out onto the highway heading for Amy, the blue Mercedes blew past us, doing about ninety. Ryan was already committed to turning, any other choice now would have caused an accident. By the time we turned around and headed after the car, all we could see was the dust it threw up due to the dry gravel on the road. It looked like the pictures of the Oklahoma dust bowl I'd seen at school.

We were flying after it, but between the dust it was kicking up and that of two cars coming toward us, we couldn't see anything. Ryan had to slow down so we didn't end up in the drainage ditch on the edge of the road. A sharp turn to the left and another immediately to the right slowed us even more. We could no longer tell where the car was. After about five miles, Ryan turned the truck around and began looking at the road as we drove. No doubt about it, we'd lost the car. The good news? We had a perimeter in which to search.

On our second pass, I wrote down the names of the roads and the numbers on all of the mailboxes. We needed to get to Amy and Derrick. I felt excited. My glass was half-full right now. Instead of knowing the car in question was somewhere in Illinois or Missouri, I could put it in a ten-square-mile area.

Amy assured us she didn't get hurt. She also let me know she didn't want to be targeted anymore and I should do nothing else until the case was solved.

Ryan wanted Amy to leave the city, either become a groupie and follow Jake while his team was on the road or go visit a long lost relative. I agreed. She said she'd think about it. Digger didn't like to fly.

By eleven o'clock, we had a Google Earth search of the area. The detail was more than I hoped for. It showed the trees in the yards, cars parked outside, and even people on the decks. I narrowed it to five places.

Ryan agreed.

It was almost dark so we opted to go searching in the morning. Meantime, there were carloads of security men up and down the road in case someone decided to make a beer and pizza run during the night.

We got back to the apartment around nine. Amy called as we were going up. "I'm going with Jake. I'll only be gone five days. Can you watch Digger? It'll give you a chance to see if you really want to take care of a dog."

"Sure, I'll come get him."

"No. We aren't leaving until tomorrow, which gives me one more night with him."

Jeez, even if I *had* a dog, I couldn't see having to sleep with it or be upset if I went on vacation and it stayed home. I really didn't get this pet thing. Was it my shortcoming?

"Okay, pack his jammies, food, and snacks and I'll get him in the morning."

"Will do. Once you get a pet of your own, you'll understand."

I shook my head. "If you say so."

"We need to talk," Ryan said.

"I don't want to, not tonight. I'm confused enough without trying to sort out my feelings about us."

"Okay. I accept that. But I don't like going home with all of this going on."

"No one's going to hurt me."

"Maybe it isn't you I'm worried about."

"You're telling me you're afraid?"

"Not exactly. I am telling you it is safer for both of us right here. Only one-way in and one-way out. Both vehicles can be watched at the same time."

I fell onto the couch as if I'd just run a half marathon. "Okay, you've made your point. You're welcome to stay. But you may find out I'm the most horrible person on earth. I don't want to get close and lose anyone else."

He sat down beside me. "Kate, you have been my choice for a very long time. I've never tried to date you or move past friendship with you, for fear I would mess it up and not have you in my life at all."

I put my hand up to his lips. "No declarations."

"It's not a declaration. It's a truth. I need to reveal it before you convince yourself how rotten you are. When you fell in love with Michael, I could see how it happened. I loved him myself. We all did. But he's gone, and you had nothing to do with it. Once you realize that, perhaps we'll have a future. Meanwhile, I'll bunk in one of the guest rooms."

I could do nothing but look at him. Once again, I felt like the short girl who couldn't reach the top shelf of her locker. The woman who had to have the airbag disconnected in her car so, if it went off, it wouldn't kill her. I was the woman who got her husband and friends killed because she was too selfish a person to help Jasmine Wu.

I began to cry. Ryan tried to console me, but I needed to get it out. Tears flowed for Michael, Roomy, and Andy, all the terror Lizzy must be going through, and Jasmine Wu and her lost career.

I fell asleep—exhausted, guilty, and sad. Ryan was still holding me when I woke up several hours later and went to bed.

CHAPTER 30

Quite a sight greeted me in the morning. I stood in front of the mirror and surveyed myself. Puffy eyes, red nose, runny mascara, and unruly red hair. How could anyone love me? I was blessed. Michael was a special man and so was Ryan. I took my hand and splashed water on the image staring at me then hopped in the shower.

Ah, the miracle of hot water.

We all had our happy places, places we retreated to when things got out of hand. One of my spots was a hot shower. I loved hot showers. By the time I was done, I felt half way normal and worthy of human kindness. I stood in my closet, looking for something to wear.

The weather was chilly in the morning, hot in the afternoon, and cooled down again in the evening. A typical spring in St. Louis. I chose tan slacks, a V-neck tee shirt in teal blue, along with a brown jacket to conceal my weapon. My hair cooperated for the first time in a month so I wore it natural. Natural for me was a mass of ringlets circling my face and running down my back. It would have to do.

Ryan wasn't in the living room or kitchen when I went in to make a cup of latte. The miracle of the Keurig allowed me to make something as good as Starbucks for less than a dollar. I wasn't one to complain about saving money.

I walked toward the guest room. The door was half closed. Without opening it, I could hear the shower in the guest bath running so I walked back to the kitchen, made a cup of coffee, and headed back to sit it on the nightstand where he could find it when he came out. Thing was, he opened the door the same time I did and stood in the door-way in nothing more than the steam from the hot water to cover him. I didn't look away. Before me stood a gorgeous man with the wide shoulders of a weight lifter, the narrow hips of a runner, and all the manhood of Zeus.

"Nice," I said, put the coffee down, and walked out.

It was the most chauvinist thing I had ever done. I won-dered what the word for misogynist was when things were turned around and the woman was the aggressor.

I enjoyed my latte as I laughed to myself. Maybe I got too much sleep.

If Ryan was embarrassed by my staring or remarks, he didn't act like it. "Thanks for the coffee. Are you ready to track down the blue Mercedes?"

"You're welcome, and I'm ready to go. We have to stop by Amy's and pick up Digger."

The ride to Amy's was uneventful. I sat lost in thought as I watched the scenery fly by but didn't really see any of it. If Ryan had anything on his mind, he didn't share it with me.

Amy had the dog packed like a kid going to camp. She had made a list for me of when to feed him and twenty-plus things to make him more comfortable. I felt like I was babysitting for Prince George. I merely smiled and put him on my lap in the truck.

In less than an hour, we were in Granite City. Digger was happy as a clam on my leg, looking out the window. We met two cars full of Ryan's men on Route 111. We pulled over and got out. I left Digger in the car. Ryan wanted one car at one end of Pogue Road and the other at the opposite end. We were going to go Mercedes hunting alone. Their only job was to let us know if the car came by them while we were off the road looking for it.

It was a long morning. We started out looking at the five places we targeted by satellite the night before. We left the truck on the road and hiked in the woods up to the edges of the yards. The first one looked abandoned. The yard had grass four feet high and trees hanging over the driveway so no one could have driven up it. We checked out the old barn to the right of the house but there was no car in sight. We headed back to the main road and the truck.

The second place was a thriving farm, complete with kids, horses, goats, cows, and a garden plot. It wasn't the sort of place we would find Lizzy.

We hit pay dirt as we walked up the fifth lane. It led to a place that looked like it was out of the old South. It'd been stately in its time. Now it was rundown and in dire need of paint and a lawn mower. There were so many trees shading it we could see lights on inside, although the sun shined brightly all around us. As soon as we saw the house, we retreated off the driveway and into the band of heavy woods surrounding it. We had plenty of cover. Ryan tapped me on the shoulder and pointed to a shed about fifty yards to our left. Cautiously we ran and hid behind it. Behind the filthy window in the back, we saw the car, a blue Mercedes with no license plate.

I sneaked to the left side of the house and Ryan went to the right. We had our guns drawn. Of course, I couldn't see in the windows. My head barely reached the sill, so I got down on my hands and knees and looked in the basement.

It was lit up like daylight down there, and Lizzy sat painting in front of one of the biggest canvases I had ever seen. She was talking to someone out of sight. I crab walked to another window and looked in. From my first vantage point, I had been able to see the back of my friend. From here, I could see her profile. Her hair looked filthy and rat-ted. I wished she would turn and look at me so I could signal to her that this was almost over.

She didn't.

I could still hear voices, so I knew she wasn't alone. I wondered what Ryan saw.

I didn't have to wonder long. He appeared near the front of the house, crouched down, and motioning for me to come his way. I was careful so as not to be seen. I crawled away from the basement and toward him.

When I was close enough, he signaled me to move away from the house. I guessed he wanted to talk. We both ran about fifty yards toward the truck and sat down at the base of a hundred year old oak tree that, on a better day, I would have liked to climb.

I leaned back and looked toward him. "What did you see?"

"Not much. There was music playing, food on the kitchen table, and I could hear voices but I didn't see anyone."

I nodded. "I saw Lizzy. She's in the basement, painting. Her hair's matted and she's dirty, but she appears okay. She didn't look at me so I couldn't let her know we were about to get her out of there."

"It's probably for the best," he said. "If you'd startled her, it could get her killed. These aren't nice people we're dealing with."

"I know, but from what I could see, she looked awful. You know we can't just go in there and get her, don't you?"

"I figured as much."

"We're in Illinois, for one thing. If we go in, it could make everything we find inadmissible in court. I don't want to have Michael's killer in my hands and lose him on a technicality."

"Not just Michael."

"I know, I'm just saying,"

"I understand." He squeezed my hand, gave me a smile, and pulled me to my feet. "Let's go back to the truck."

We thought it best to move away from the house, in case someone decided to leave. At the corner, we met the men monitoring who came and went. Ryan told them to park across the highway on a grassy knoll he pointed to and watch for the car. If it left, they were to follow it. I called the guards in the car stationed at the other end of the road and asked them if they could be inconspicuous and they said yes. Ten minutes later, we were on our way to Central and Roger Simon's office. I was giddy, nervous, and scared for my friend.

On the way to St. Louis, I thought back on all that had happened. Soon I would know if it was because I didn't help Jasmine Wu at the Jump Club. It reminded me of Digger who had jumped back on my lap. We pulled over and I took him for a short walk, gave him a treat, and a drink of water. If he missed Amy, he didn't act like it.

~ ~ ~

We waited fifteen minutes for Roger to come back from lunch. Mostly, my stomach ruled me. This was a rare occasion. Food was secondary to settling this case. Could I be growing up? I doubted it. I would be thirty-three on May first. Birthdays were not as exciting as they once were.

Roger walked in while I was deep in thought. Ryan had stepped out to make a phone call.

If he was surprised I was there, he didn't show it. "Hi there, what's up?"

"I think we found Lizzy Smith. Well, no, I'm sure we found Lizzy Smith."

"Where is she?"

Ryan walked in and sat in a chair near the door. I thought he didn't want to talk so as not to steal my thunder.

"She's in a house in Pogue, off Route 111 and 270, outside of Granite City."

"How did you find her?"

I spent the next half an hour filling him in on the Jump Club fire, Stanley Wu, Jasmine, and her accident, Lizzy knowing both of them from the Kansas City Art Institute, and, worst of all, the fact that I let Jasmine remain trapped under a table—perhaps longer than need be, because I didn't insist the paramedic come immediately.

Once I finished my story, Roger sat quietly as if trying to take it all in. "Sounds as if you've busted this wide open. I'll get a hold of the Illinois Highway Patrol and the Madison County Sheriff and see if they will let us have a part in our own case."

He was on the phone for over an hour. He had a three-way conversation going with the sheriff, the captain, and the Granite City Police, who said they would love to be in on it but it was out of their jurisdiction. Roger keyed open his phone at the beginning of the call so Ryan and I heard everything. We were to meet at the Madison County Sheriff's office in one hour.

It was finally going to happen. We would catch the bad guys—Stanley Wu, or someone who worked for him—free Lizzy, and stop the killing and mayhem for good.

We took Ryan's truck and followed Roger and three of his men. We got there five minutes early. "Kate, you're a civilian here. I know you want to be in on all of this, but I can't guarantee you the Illinois troops will agree it's safe."

When we arrived, we were told the FBI had been notified because Lizzy was from Missouri and apparently had been transported to Illinois. This thing was getting bigger. Within thirty minutes, four agents from the Springfield, Illinois, office walked in the door. So now, there were eighteen of us. We had enough manpower and firepower to overthrow a small country.

The FBI had maps of the area, Ryan and I made notes, drew pictures, and pointed out hiding places from the road to the house. Everyone was nice to us but they were clear, unless someone shot directly at us, we were to stay in the background. We nodded our heads in agreement, although I knew neither one of us actually did.

By four in the afternoon, we headed toward Pogue.

They sent two men in camo outfits with a thermo-imaging camera up the lane to see how many people were in the house. They came back puzzled, saying they heard conversation yet picked up only one heat-image. We all decided it was strange.

We spread out and headed toward the house. The FBI were on the south; the highway patrol on the north; the sheriff and his men headed east; and Roger, his men, Ryan, and I walked up the west side. It was familiar because it was the route we took the first time we were there.

As preplanned, when we got to the shed, we signaled that the car was still parked inside.

After that, it all happened fast. On a predetermined signal, men went in the front and back doors. They swarmed the house and the basement and, within minutes, came out and motioned for us to come in.

There was an FBI agent talking quietly with Roger. They came over to us. Roger spoke first. "Kate, there's no good way to say this. Things are not as we thought they were. I don't know what to say here to prepare you for what you're about to see."

"Is Lizzy dead?"

"No, but she hasn't been kidnapped either. I'm going to take you downstairs, but you have to promise me you'll stay calm."

I was anything but calm. I didn't have an imagination big enough to try to come up with anything to match the horror on Roger and the agents' faces.

The sheriff came upstairs. "The medical examiner's on the way. Ms. Nash, you can go down now. We have Miss Smith restrained. You know the drill, please refrain from touching anything."

Ryan took my arm, and we headed toward the basement door. I looked back. Roger was deep in conversation with the men around him, and everyone was shaking their heads in disbelief.

Oh, my goodness! There was such a mess in the basement. My eyes flitted from place to place, but I couldn't stay focused on any one thing. My mind wanted to explode, and my eyes wanted to look away.

This was what I saw: Lizzy was handcuffed to the rail of the bed she was sitting on. Her hair hung matted and filthy onto her sagging shoulders. She stared at me but her eyes were glazed and glassy. I didn't think she could focus. She looked at something behind me, over my shoulder.

When I turned around, I let out a gasp. It was something nearly indescribable. I thought it used to be a human. It was Jasmine Wu. It sat on a platform about two feet off the floor. I knew it was Jasmine because its legs were missing. The thing was dressed in ski gear from the waist up. It's hair was thick, black, and shiny. There was make up on the face— almost clown like—and the skin was dark, mummy looking. I fought back the bile rising in my throat.

I looked at Ryan. He was white as his eyes scanned the room until they found mine. "Are you okay?"

I couldn't get my mind around it. "What are we looking at?"

"We'll talk later," he said.

I kept looking around. There were paintings everywhere, at least fifty of them. They were of the hideous thing on the stand, but they looked more like Jasmine might have looked alive. The rest of the paintings I recognized to be by Jasmine Wu, the painter. It was too bizarre for me to comprehend.

I took three big steps toward Lizzy who, until this time, showed no signs of life or spunk. As I got within her reach, she jumped up and grabbed my neck with her free arm.

"You bitch! You murdering, unfeeling bitch. You took my life from me, and this is what I get." Had it not been that one of her hands was handcuffed to the bed, I think she would have killed me right then.

Men came bounding down the stairs and, at the same time, Ryan hit her arm so hard, I heard it crack. She dropped her arm and fell back on the bed, giving out long moaning screams like a dying animal.

I retreated toward the stairs. "What does she mean? I didn't kill anyone."

"Let's go. We'll sort it out later."

I didn't look back, but I saw Ryan look over his shoulder.

We sat on a couch in a nicely decorated room to the left of the kitchen. Someone found some tea and fixed me a cup. I sat holding the cup in both of my shaking hands as we waited for the officers to finish their investigation.

The medical examiner was a woman, Tiffany Marshall, a no-nonsense yet compassionate woman who took her time with Lizzy and the body downstairs. The sun had set long ago and every light in the house was on when she came into the room where I sat. "That looks good. Is there any more tea around? I could use a stiff drink, but I'll settle for a hot cup of whatever she's having."

A young deputy said he would take care of it. It took two men to load Lizzy into a squad car. She fought and scratched like a feral cat. I didn't know where they were taking her. I hoped to a hospital.

Within a few minutes, the room filled up with lawmen. They leaned on walls and sat on every flat surface. It looked more like story hour at the kids' library than a crime scene. *Let's face it. No one had ever seen anything like this.*

It was the stuff of nightmares for years to come, and we all wanted to know what happened.

"As near as I can tell," the medical examiner said, "Jasmine Wu died about three years ago. I'm going to speculate on some of this and, when I get all of the chemical analysis back from the lab, I'll fill in the parts where I might have guessed wrong. Your friend didn't take the death well. I would say they were more than friends. Rather than not have Miss Wu in her life, Miss Smith varnished her body. By the looks of it, I'd say there were twenty or thirty coats of the stuff. I'm guessing, from the initial decay, before she came up with her plan to preserve her friend, she let her lay a few days. Her hair has several cans of hair spray on it. Miss Smith didn't realize that hair doesn't rot, and it was something she need not have done.

"Looks like, over the last year or so, Miss Smith has been painting portrait after portrait of Miss Wu, depicting the beauty she had in life. Your friend, Lizzy Smith, is a mental case. The death of her soul mate—and I am only guessing that was their relationship—was more than her mind could handle. That's about all I can tell you for now. Miss Smith will remain at Alton Memorial Hospital for observation. I'll have a full report in a week or two."

I sat, staring in disbelief. Ryan told her thanks. He walked over and said he thought it was time for us to go. We walked silently to the truck, where Digger was jumping up and down like a wild man. He had been in the truck for several hours. He missed dinner and probably needed a potty break. I put his lead on him and started walking down the road. Ryan started the truck and followed slowly behind. We fed the dog and gave him water. While we drove back to the city, I held that puppy as if he was the most important thing in the world to me. Maybe I did need a dog. They certainly were more forgiving than people were.

CHAPTER 31

It had been three weeks since the day at the farm. Amy was back and we had tackled several new cases. Life was good, if you didn't count my guilt over Lizzy, Michael, Roomy, and Andy. Ryan said I was too hard on myself. I asked for forgiveness daily and didn't even kill a spider anymore. I relocated them to the balcony or took them downstairs.

Tiffany Marshall finished her report and sent a copy to Roger's office. He invited Ryan, Amy, and me in to read it. While we were there, we read all the investigative notes they were making for the case they filed against Lizzy. She was charged with the murders of Michael, Roomy, Andy, Doug and the theft of some twenty paintings from Wu Enterprises.

Just for good measure, they charged her with the attempted murder of Amy, Ryan, and me. One conviction would send her to prison for life, but she freely admitted to all of it in gory detail, blaming me for ruining her life because I didn't move fast enough to help Jasmine at the scene of the fire.

Four separate medical experts testified that the paramedics would not have come any sooner had I pleaded and begged. There were too many injured people and not enough emergency personal. I was guilty of one thing only, and that was not staying with Jasmine and comforting her, during the hour or so she waited.

Each doctor agreed that Jasmine's legs were crushed when the table went airborne and hit them and a steel beam from the ceiling added to the weight. They said there was no way I could have helped her.

It didn't make me feel any better. Holding her hand would have been the humane thing to do.

Lizzy told the court she intended to kill me, but she wanted to hurt me first, thus the murders of my friends and the attempts on the others.

The morning she left the message for me to meet her in the park, she was going to kidnap me and take me to the farm with her and Jasmine. She had waited for hours to make sure no one was there. She waited too long and showed up the same time Ryan did. It saved my life.

The night we saw her stealing paintings from the warehouse, and we didn't think she was alone, she drove the car for a block from the passenger's side in order to throw anyone off who might think she was alone.

When she called and said she *couldn't do this anymore*, it was a brief moment of sanity.

She had gone to the Wiccan Coven, hoping she could have a baby for her and dead Jasmine to raise. Thank goodness that part of her plan didn't work.

When we left the station, I felt dirty and guilty. Ryan and Amy tried to comfort me. I had wondered many times why I didn't stay with Jasmine. The only reason I had was that I was looking for my family, and that included Lizzy. I had gone over that night a thousand times, and I remembered that I went back to Jasmine no less than ten times during that hour.

~ ~ ~

I wanted to be alone.

Ryan took Amy home and then me. He left me at the door and didn't even ask to come up.

What did I do now? Maybe it was me who was crazy. When he wanted to stay, I pushed him away, and when he tried to do the right thing, I wanted him.

Ah.

After a half a bottle of wine and a hot bath, I went to bed and slept like the dead. I woke up to a strange noise and a cold something on my nose. I opened my eyes to loving brown ones staring back at me and warm puppy breath. "Ryan, Amy, Are you guys here?" More kisses on my face and then some burrowing under the covers. It was a puppy. "Hi, little guy," I picked it up. "Oops, I mean, little girl."

I cuddled her and went into the kitchen. There was a small dog kennel, a water bowl, food, treats, and a note. *My name is Chili. I am a miniature dachshund, and I am your forever friend. No matter what you do, I will always love you.*

I went into the living room, puppy in hand, and there sat Ryan. He patted the seat next to him. "Do you like her?"

"She's beautiful. I don't think I'm ready to have a puppy, though."

"Sure you are. She and I are going to teach you all about unconditional love. And I know you're ready for that."

The End

About the Author

Susan Keene was born in California and raised in Illinois. She spent twenty years in the medical profession and loves to weave her experiences into the books she writes.

Besides helping to create a workshop for beginning writers, she is an officer in Sleuth's Ink Mystery Writers and a member of Ozarks Romance Authors.

She loves speaking to children and young adults about writing as a career. This year she will join the Annual Children's Literary Festival of the Ozarks, held at Missouri State University, as a speaker and mentor.

Keene lives on a farm in the beautiful Ozarks, where she and her family raise cattle, sheep, apples, and pears. Her current work, *Who's Roxie Watkins?* is the second book in her Kate Nash mystery series.